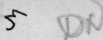 

Viktor looked down at his crying son.

He was so little. Viktor's hand was as big as the baby's whole head.

"Can I see him?" Kat asked, quietly.

He started to lift the baby from the bed. His hands were awkward, so big and clumsy. He couldn't shake the feeling that if he didn't place his hands perfectly, he'd hurt the baby.

A weight bore down on Viktor's chest, making it hard for his heart to keep its beat. Ever since he'd learned the rebels had discovered Kat's whereabouts, he'd lived with the overwhelming fear that she would be hurt. Killed. He'd been sure that no feeling could be worse.

He wasn't ready for this.

Staring down at this little creature, holding the squirming body in his hands, Viktor's whole being ached like an open wound. A wound that he knew instinctively would never heal.

And for the first time in his life, he understood what it was like to be truly afraid.

Dear Reader,

I'm delighted to be part of Harlequin's 60th anniversary celebration. In the DIAMONDS AND DADDIES miniseries, I had the privilege of working with three very creative authors—Rita Herron, Dana Marton and Elle James—and we had a great time. Working with other authors always reminds me of playing pretend with my friends when I was a child. I hope the series gives you as much enjoyment as we had creating it.

Priceless Newborn Prince gave me the chance to write about two very special things in my life: horses and children. I worked with horses for years, starting with training and showing my own quarter horse, Bonanza's Copy Cat. Later I worked for trainers and traveled all over the country helping them compete in shows such as the Quarter Horse Congress in Columbus, Ohio, and the World Championship Quarter Horse Show in Oklahoma City. I've always wanted to bring some of my horse experience into a novel, and this project was the perfect fit.

The other important experience I was able to explore in *Priceless Newborn Prince* was childbirth. There are few moments in a mother's life as fraught with pain and joy as bringing a child into the world. It was rewarding to be able to draw on my own experiences to tell Viktor and Kat's story. And of course, having children doesn't stop with birth. I think we all have to remember that our actions today determine what kind of future our children and grandchildren will have tomorrow. Let's make their futures something of which we can be proud.

I hope you enjoy reading *Priceless Newborn Prince!*

Sincerely,

Ann Voss Peterson

ANN VOSS PETERSON

PRICELESS NEWBORN PRINCE

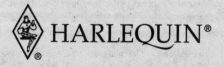

HARLEQUIN®

TORONTO • NEW YORK • LONDON
AMSTERDAM • PARIS • SYDNEY • HAMBURG
STOCKHOLM • ATHENS • TOKYO • MILAN • MADRID
PRAGUE • WARSAW • BUDAPEST • AUCKLAND

To Cole and Brett.
Special thanks to Rita, Dana and Elle
for making this series a lot of fun, and to
Denise and Allison for a great opportunity.

Recycling programs
for this product may
not exist in your area.

ISBN-13: 978-0-373-88907-5
ISBN-10:   0-373-88907-0

PRICELESS NEWBORN PRINCE

Copyright © 2009 by Ann Voss Peterson

www.eHarlequin.com

Printed in U.S.A.

ABOUT THE AUTHOR

Ever since she was a little girl making her own books out of construction paper, Ann Voss Peterson wanted to write. So when it came time to choose a major at the University of Wisconsin, creative writing was her only choice. Of course, writing wasn't a *practical* choice—one needs to earn a living. So Ann found jobs ranging from proofreading legal transcripts to working with quarter horses to washing windows. But no matter how she earned her paycheck, she continued to write the type of stories that captured her heart and imagination—romantic suspense. Ann lives near Madison, Wisconsin, with her husband, her two young sons, her border collie and her quarter horse mare. Ann loves to hear from readers. E-mail her at ann@annvosspeterson.com or visit her Web site at www.annvosspeterson.com.

Books by Ann Voss Peterson

CAST OF CHARACTERS

Viktor Romanov—The prince of Rasnovia has spent his life doing what's best for his fledgling country. But when a rebel coup kills his parents and leaves him for dead, he must do everything he can to protect his secret love and unborn son.

Kat Edwards—Nine months pregnant and desperate to protect her child, Kat is overjoyed when Viktor comes back from the dead to help her.

Daniel Romanov—The priceless newborn prince is as much of a threat to the Rasnovian rebellion as his father.

Lawrence McElroy—The wealthy horseman has a bone to pick with Viktor and his friends. Is he bitter enough to finance the rebellion? Or is he just greedy?

Amal Jabar—The Middle Eastern businessman has shady connections and a building resentment toward the Aggie Four. How far would he go to see them cut down to size?

Deke Norton—A friend and colleague of the Aggie Four who offers them business advice, but could he secretly resent them for leaving him out of their tight foursome?

Warren Gregory—An economic hit man, Warren specializes in the economic takeover of developing countries.

Deputy Bobby Lee Stubfield—A law officer on the take. But does he have a personal grudge, too?

Special Agent Ross Keller—The FBI agent knows something shady is going on.

The Aggie Four—Not merely a group of friends and business partners, **Flint McKade, Akeem Abdul, Jackson Champion** and **Viktor Romanov** would die for each other. Will they have to?

Chapter One

Kat Edwards didn't recognize the men, but she knew why they were there.

She hadn't heard them enter the barn, not above the whir of the horse clipper and jangle of country music on the radio. If she had, she could have run. She could have hidden in one of the stalls. Something. Now all she could do was watch them stride toward her, grim expressions on coarse-featured faces. Their hands swung empty by their sides, but the telltale bulges under their shirttails said it all.

They'd come to kill her baby.

She brought her free hand to her round abdomen, as if she could shield her little prince from trouble with mere flesh and bone. She needed to do something. But what? She couldn't scream for help. She was the only groom still in the barn. The only one who'd had to take a nap this afternoon and as a result hadn't yet finished her work. No one would venture back into the barn until it was time for night check. Hours away. She was on her own.

She couldn't make a run for it, could she? She was as big as the barn itself, nearly nine months along. Even if they gave her an opening, how fast could she move?

She needed a weapon.

She turned off the clipper, and concentrated on its weight in her hand, the sharp teeth of the blades. It wouldn't do much damage beyond giving her assailant a nasty scratch. She had to find something better or she didn't stand a chance.

"Katherine Edwards?" the bigger one said, his thick accent slicing into her name. Not the Rasnovian lilt she'd been expecting. Something more brutal. Maybe German.

She gave the men the most blasé expression she could muster. "Katherine? You missed her. Sorry."

As if sensing tension in the air, the sorrel colt she'd been clipping tossed his head, rattling the cross ties that held him.

She smoothed a hand over his slick coat and took mental inventory of the other grooming tools around her. The hoof pick was metal, but not terribly sharp. And not useful unless she was close enough to sink the end into an eye. The brushes were no good. Neither was the horse vac. She could hardly lift that. If only she'd been cleaning stalls when they found her. At least then she'd have a manure fork.

The men's steps slowed as they drew nearer. The shorter one focused a stare on her belly. His eyes drilled into her, cold and hard, like the bullet that would probably follow.

She splayed her hands out in front of her. "Look, I don't know why you're here, and I don't know what kind of trouble Katherine has gotten herself in. But I'm telling you, I'm not her."

They stopped fifteen feet away and watched her through narrowed eyes.

Maybe all the lying practice she'd gotten in her rebellious teen years was paying off. At least enough to buy her some time. Give her a chance to figure a way out of this mess. "Listen, she's probably in her apartment. Just go out the way you came and take a left. I'd bring you there myself, but I can't leave this colt standing in cross ties."

"Put him in a stall." The taller one stepped closer. The other one drifted to one side, as if positioning himself to cut off any possible escape route.

So much for buying time. And she still hadn't come up with an answer. Soon it would be all over. She and her baby would be dead. She needed to think.

The colt jigged in place, then pawed the thick

rubber mat under his feet. He sensed something was going on, and he didn't like it one bit. Powerful muscles coiled under his satin coat, ready to explode.

Her gaze landed on a soft cotton lead rope with a heavy steel snap on one end. Not the greatest of weapons, but she could no longer afford to be picky. She set down the clipper and picked up the rope. "All right. I'll put him away and show you to the apartments." She clipped the lead rope to the colt's halter and reached for a cross tie.

She wasn't ready for the pain.

It ignited in her back, a spark like the strike of a match. Tendons tightened. Muscles contracted. Fingers of pressure wrapped around her middle, centering low in her belly.

Not now.

She fought the urge to groan, to lean forward and rest her hands on her thighs. She needed to stay focused on the men. She needed to find a way out.

The tall one's hand hovered closer to the bulge under his shirttail. "What are you waiting for?"

"Nothing." Gritting her teeth against the contraction, she reached the cross tie on one side and released the snap. Then she reached for the other. She turned the colt, positioning his body between her and the men. The two-year-old tossed his head, yanking at the rope, eager to return to his stall on the other side of the men.

The pain around her middle started to withdraw, pulling back until a cramp in her lower back was all that was left.

It was now or never.

She grasped the lead rope's snap, her sweaty fingers slick on the cool metal. She pulled it open and let the colt do the rest.

He launched off the rubber mat. Steel shoes clattered on concrete. Swerving to the side, he headed for the open door of his stall. The men scrambled to get out of his way. His hip plowed into the taller man, sending him sprawling to his knees.

Kat whirled and ran.

She focused on the double door at the end of the barn's long corridor and raced straight for it. Her leg muscles pumped. Her abdominal muscles strained with each stride. She clamped one hand over her belly, trying to hold some of the weight, willing her legs to move faster.

Her pulse drummed in her ears, but over the frantic beat she could hear the shorter man, still on his feet, boots thundering behind. Drawing closer.

She wasn't going to make it.

His breath rasped over her shoulder. His hand closed around her arm. Brutal fingers dug into her flesh.

She stopped and spun. The lead rope flew around her in an arc. The heavy steel snap smacked into the side of his head.

Curses flew from his lips. American.

Kat didn't wait to listen. She wrenched her arm away and pushed the last few yards.

He was after her before she made it. His footfalls slapped heavy on the concrete. Another set joined in. The taller man, up and running.

She clawed at the sliding door. Throwing her weight to the side, she yanked with all her strength. It inched open. Slowly. Too slowly.

A shout echoed through the barn behind her. A crack of gunfire shattered the air. The blast bounced off concrete. Loud, so loud. Horses thumped against the walls of their stalls and shrieked in panic.

She pushed herself through the opening, bracing herself, sure she'd feel a bullet tearing through her or a hand gripping her arm. She burst outside and ran for all she was worth. Gravel crunched and skittered under her boots. Behind her, another shot fired and another, sounding more like the loud pop of a cap gun now that she was outside.

She kept her legs moving. She had to get away, to hide. But where? The driveway and a small parking area for horse trailers stretched straight in front of her. Steel pipe turnout pens flanked either side of the drive. There was no way she'd fit between the rails, and as big as she was, she doubted she could climb over.

Another shot. And another. Panicked whinnies reached a crescendo.

She raced for the two horse trailers she and others had spent the afternoon readying for the trip to Akeem's auction house. It wouldn't be hard for the men to guess where she'd gone, but if she could arm herself and be ready for them, maybe she'd have a fighting chance.

She passed the first trailer, a small model built for four, and moved on to the six-horse slant. She knew the tack compartment was filled with bales of alfalfa and bags of rolled oats. No room to hide. Bypassing it, she climbed the steps to the larger dressing room and let herself inside.

Still, muggy air closed around her. Darkness swam in front of her. She groped in the narrow space, willing her eyes to adjust. Even though she had organized the grooming supplies, tack and other equipment jamming the space just hours ago, she struggled to remember what was what in the dark.

Outside the trailer, the shooting seemed to have stopped. All she could hear were a few frightened screams from the horses and the occasional thunk of hooves on the wooden stalls.

She didn't know who the men had been

shooting at, but the silence could only mean one thing. Whoever had won the firefight would be coming after her. She could only pray it wasn't the men who wanted her baby dead.

She squinted in the darkness. She could make out the silhouettes of silver halters, bridles and saddles that would be used to show off the horses to prospective bidders. The tack trunk hulked at the back of the dressing room, and next to it leaned a large, two-wheeled cart.

Heart thumping, she tipped the cart back and groped for the manure fork she knew was tucked underneath. Her fingers closed around the slick, wood handle. The angled fork was made of plastic. Not the best of weapons, but at least she wasn't empty-handed. They weren't going to get her and her baby without a fight.

The whoosh of the barn door sliding along its track filtered into the trailer.

She gripped the fork and pulled it free. She needed to find the high ground. A place where she wouldn't be spotted right away. A place she could lash out with the fork. One side of the dressing room rose to a long shelf formed by the portion called the gooseneck that reached out over the pickup bed and hitched truck to trailer.

That would do.

She shoved piles of gear aside and placed her

palms on the prickly indoor/outdoor carpeting lining the space. Using all her strength, she jumped. Her arms shook as she pulled her belly over the edge and hefted herself up onto the shelf. Winded from the effort, she crouched next to the wall and tried to blend in with a pile of extra horse blankets.

Sweat slicked her skin and stung her eyes. Her back tightened.

Once again, the contraction wrapped around her from back to front. Gripping. Seizing. She gasped in a breath. She leaned forward, pressing the fork down on her thighs.

The crunch of a boot on dry gravel pricked her spine. She could hear the tack compartment squeak open, then close. The dressing room's door latch rattled.

Pressing back farther into the gooseneck, she tried to quiet her breathing, but her rapid pant roared in her ears, nearly as loud as her pulse. Gripping the wooden handle in moist palms, she steeled herself against the squeeze in her lower belly as bit by bit, it started to fade.

The door inched open. The yard light streamed into the trailer, casting a hulking shadow across a silver-trimmed saddle. A man, tall and broad-shouldered.

She lifted the fork. She had to focus. She'd only get one shot.

A foot mounted the metal step. A dark figure pushed inside. He turned slowly, scanning the jumble of equipment, searching for her. The glow from outside illuminated the side of his face.

The face of a ghost.

A whimper lodged deep in Kat's throat. Shivers shook her to the core and fanned out over her skin. The sandy-brown hair. The strong jaw. The piercing blue eyes. It couldn't be. It wasn't possible.

"Kat." His British-tinged accent washed over her.

Taking the fork from her hand, he guided her down to him. He pulled her against his solid chest and encircled her in strong arms.

She almost cried out at the feel of him. She drew in his scent, a mix of leather and sandalwood. Long lost emotions balled in her chest, squeezing her heart, making it difficult to breathe.

His embrace lasted only a second. Hands on her arms, he pushed her back a few inches and stared into her eyes. "There's no time. We have to get out of here. Now."

Kat shook her head. She felt dizzy. Like she was in a dream. Yet the man touching her was real. His scent, his voice, they were no memories this time. Viktor. Real. Here.

None of this made sense. "I thought you were dead…. I felt…"

He grasped her hand and pulled her toward the dressing room's door. "Don't think. Don't feel. Just run."

Chapter Two

God, he'd missed her.

Viktor pulled Kat across the gravel parking area and toward the pipe-fenced corral. He needed to get her away from the barn and the men inside. He had to focus on getting her to safety. But all his mind could absorb was the feel of the fine bones of her fingers gripping his, her gentle floral scent, blended with the scent of horse and Show Sheen, so light and sweet in the humid night…and the full sway of her belly as she ran.

She'd told him she was pregnant in Rasnovia, before the rebellion, before the coup, before the explosion that killed nearly everyone he loved. He'd been happy. Delirious, really. But on some level he hadn't quite believed it was real. And now…

Don't think. Don't feel. Just run.

He half lifted her, helping her scale the fence. Once on the other side, they continued running, heading for the fence on the far side and the lights twinkling beyond.

"Those men…" She cupped her free arm across her belly. "They want to kill the baby, don't they? Just like they killed your family. Just like they killed y—" Her voice hiccuped in a sob. "God, Viktor, I thought you were dead."

"I know." His throat felt thick, his chest tight. He'd known the report of his death would hit her hard. He'd wanted to tell her he survived. He'd wanted to explain. But he couldn't. Not then, and not yet. "We'll talk later. When there's time. I'll tell you everything. Now we need to get out of here."

She glanced back, as if expecting to find the men hot on their heels.

"They aren't following. But there will be others. We need help."

"How did you get here?"

"I hitchhiked." He knew he'd regret not having a vehicle, but he hadn't exactly been able to walk up to a car dealership and buy one. Not without so much as a driver's license. And with the soldiers closing in on Kat, he hadn't a second to lose procuring false identification. He'd barely made it in time as it was.

At least he knew where he could get transportation now.

They reached the fence on the other side of the

corral. Hands on her waist, he boosted her over, then scaled the steel pipe himself. Across a wide lawn rimmed in palm trees, neatly trimmed shrubs and a few late summer flowers, hulked the Diamondback Ranch's main house. They approached it from the back. Lights shone from windows on the first and second floors.

Flint was home.

Viktor didn't know how his long-time friend would react to seeing him alive. But he knew the Texan would help. If there was anyone in the world he could trust, it was the group of men he'd met as an undergraduate student at Texas A&M University, the men with whom he'd forged a brotherhood, the men who'd shared his dreams for the country of Rasnovia and pitched in to make them reality. Flint McKade, Akeem Abdul and Jackson Champion.

The men who, with him, formed The Aggie Four.

An outside light illuminated the home's spacious decks and patios.

So much for sneaking in the back way. If there were more of the rebels' men already on the ranch—and Viktor would be very surprised if there weren't—he didn't want to risk entering into that circle of light.

Clutching Kat's hand, he led her around the edge of the yard. The front was dark, only the curves of walks, flower beds and landscaping plants visible in the faint glow of the moon and illumination from the windows. He scanned the shapes of bushes and groupings of trees. Nothing out of place met his eye. He could detect no sound of movement. So far, so good.

They flanked the open space of the yard, approaching the front door from the side. Viktor stopped, sure he heard something. The rustling of a bush. The crunch of tires on gravel. All he could detect was Kat's light exhale and the normal night sounds of insects. They stepped onto the porch and pressed the doorbell.

The chime echoed through the house. Footsteps thunked from inside, cowboy boots crossing hardwood floor. The porch light flicked on, spotlighting them as if they were standing center stage.

So much for his plans of a stealthy entrance.

He scanned the landscaping again, but the light made the surrounding bushes and trees fade into dark shadow, along with any possible threat.

Open the door, Flint.

A prickle moved over his skin and raised hairs on the back of his neck. Someone was watching them. He could feel it. He just prayed it was Flint sizing up his late-night visitor and not a sniper lining them up in his sights.

Now, Flint. Open up.

The latch rattled. The door inched open. Flint McKade's broad shoulders blocked the space. He stared at them, his face blanching white under the brim of a gray felt Stetson. He opened his mouth, then closed it again. A sheen glistened in his eyes.

Viktor swallowed into a tight throat. "Flint, I need your help."

The cowboy didn't speak, didn't move.

"Please, Flint. May we come in?"

The rancher nodded haltingly, as if struggling to put all the pieces of the puzzle together in his mind. Finally he stepped back from the doorway, his usual easy amble stiff and robotic.

Quickly, Viktor ushered Kat into the foyer and closed the door behind them. Flint didn't move, he merely stared as if still uncertain what he was seeing. Kat, too, looked shell-shocked, her skin pale. The razor-cut fringes of hair framing her face were dark with perspiration.

Viktor pulled in a breath of air-conditioned air. He wished there was something he could say to make this easier for both of them. No, for *all* of them. Once he had time, he could tell them the whole story, explain why he'd made the decisions he had. But time was in short supply. Right now, they didn't have a moment to lose. "I shot some men in one of your barns. I need you to call the sheriff's department and an ambulance."

Flint's brows slanted low. "I heard gunfire. But let me get this straight, you shot some *men?*"

"Mercenary soldiers. Two of them. Hired by the thugs who've taken over the Rasnovian government."

His confused expression hardened, as if his mind and emotions had caught up to what he was seeing and were starting to jump ahead. "Oh, you must mean the thugs who assassinated the entire royal family. Including *you.*"

"I can explain. I will once I can be sure Kat is safe."

"Kat?" Flint looked at her as if he'd never really seen her before, even though she'd been working at his ranch for months. Finally, his gaze strayed from her face and rested on her belly. His eyes shot back to Viktor. "Yours?"

"Yes." He squeezed Kat's hand, but kept his attention on Flint.

The cowboy tilted his hat back and rubbed his forehead. "I'll be damned. The unborn heir to the throne. Right here on my ranch."

"We don't have time to hash this out. My sources say they sent a lot more than two men to the States to find Kat. They might be here in the Houston area. Maybe already on the ranch. I need your help, Flint."

Flint looked him dead in the eye. "Help? So now you trust me?"

Viktor hadn't seen Flint truly angry very often in all the years they'd been friends. But it didn't take multiple graduate degrees to recognize his friend was angry now. And Viktor certainly couldn't blame him. "Of course, I trust you."

"You didn't in February. I could have helped then. We all could have helped. Me, Akeem, Jackson. You let us believe you were dead." The cowboy's eyes narrowed. His gaze flicked to Kat, then back to Viktor. "No. That's not the way it went down, was it? Maybe you let me and Jackson believe you were dead. But Akeem brought Kat here. Akeem knew."

Viktor nodded. He could feel Kat's stare. It burned into him as fiercely as Flint's.

Flint shook his head. "Damn that Akeem. I understand you being an independent fool. You were always a little like that. But I would have thought Akeem had a better head on his shoulders."

"Akeem had no choice. I made him swear to secrecy."

"I need a drink, damn it." Flint added a few more words to the curse, then spun and paced across the floor. The heels of his boots drummed the hardwood. He stopped short of the bar and grabbed a cordless phone from its charger. He thrust the device at Viktor.

Viktor held up a hand, palm out. "I'm dead. I'd prefer to stay that way, at least for now."

"How about the men in the barn? Do they know the Prince of Rasnovia was the one who shot them?"

Viktor flinched inside at the bitter way his friend spat his title. Although Flint had put his feelings aside to help them, he was still angry. And the worst part was that Viktor couldn't blame him. If he was in Flint's place, he'd feel the same way. "I doubt they saw my face well enough to recognize me. I'm not even sure if they're still alive."

Viktor didn't want to think too hard about the possibility that he might have just killed someone. Although he was an accomplished marksman, Rasnovia didn't have a real military, and he had never been a soldier. He'd never had to face a situation like he had tonight, not even in the form of training exercises. All he'd done was what he had to in order to save Kat's life.

Flint punched in 911. He explained to the dispatcher that there had been a shooting without giving details and asked that deputies and an ambulance be sent to the ranch. Cutting off the call, he tossed the phone onto the bar and picked up a bottle of whiskey. He held the bottle in midair for a moment, then with a heavy sigh, he set the booze back down. "Damn, Viktor. After all we've been through…you should've known we'd move the blasted Rasnovian mountains to help."

"You did help, Flint. That's why I asked Akeem

to bring Kat to the Diamondback. I knew you'd give her a job. I knew you'd watch out for her."

"Might have been easier if I'd known who she was. Might have been easier on all of us if we'd known you were still alive. We had a memorial service for you. We were…" He frowned and averted his gaze. "Damn it, Viktor."

"I'm sorry. If I could have done it differently, I would have." And he meant it. Every word.

Flint's expression was hard, emotionless, but Viktor could tell now that his friend had processed the fact that he was still alive, he had the urge to take Viktor apart piece by piece for his deception. Instead, he pulled in a shuddering breath and focused on Kat. "*You* could have told me."

"I didn't know." Kat's voice was low, barely above a whisper.

A pang hit Viktor in the center of his chest. He'd wanted to tell her, most of all. But he knew that would only bring the danger he faced down on her…and on their unborn child.

He let his gaze rest for a moment on her belly. His baby. Their baby. The thought still made him feel slightly off balance. "I'll explain. All of it. I promise. Right now, I need to get Kat out of here."

"You need a truck?"

"I would be very grateful."

"What else? You have a gun."

Viktor patted the holster on his belt that held the 9 mm he'd bought illegally in Mexico before he'd sneaked across the border into the States.

"You need a—" Flint frowned and looked past Viktor. "Not so fast."

Viktor turned and followed Flint's line of sight.

He hadn't heard Kat fade back to the seating area, but now she sat perched on the edge of a sofa cushion. Arms low around her belly, she hunched forward, breathing hard.

For a second, Viktor's mind froze.

"Looks like you're going to be a daddy, Viktor," Flint said. All shades of anger gone, his voice was soft and rough with a very different kind of emotion. "I'll get Lora Leigh."

Viktor heard Flint's boots cross the foyer and head up the stairs, but all he could see was Kat. He was by her side before he realized he'd decided to move. "You're having contractions?"

Blowing heavy breaths through tight lips, she nodded. "Third one."

"What can I do?" He reached out a hand, but she didn't take it. She just hunched forward and breathed, as if he wasn't there.

He knelt down beside her. He'd prepared all his life to lead his country into democracy. He was used to being in charge, in control. Since the coup, he'd been mired in a special kind of hell for months. He hadn't been in control of anything. But he'd never felt as helpless as he did right now.

Footsteps thumped down the staircase. A petite blonde wrapped in a white terrycloth robe raced into the room, followed by Flint. She went straight to Kat, sat on the sofa beside her and took her hand. "It's okay, honey. Just keep breathing like we practiced. Everything's okay."

Kat breathed a few more seconds, then slowly straightened. "I'm…I'm okay."

Viktor let out a sigh, but no feeling of relief chased it. His sources in Rasnovia had said the rebels had a contact in Houston. Someone who had figured out who Kat was. Someone who could keep an eye on her, knew how to get to her. Viktor had to get her out of here. He had to take her somewhere no one could find her. And how on earth could he do that when she was going to have a baby?

He studied the blonde. "Lora Leigh?"

She nodded. "I've heard a lot about you, Viktor."

He gave her a brief smile he hoped would smooth over his lack of manners. "Are you a doctor?"

"A veterinarian."

Unfortunate. "We need to find a doctor."

"I don't know," Kat mumbled under her breath. "That contraction felt like I might be giving birth to a foal."

Lora Leigh gave a laugh. "Keep your humor through this, girl, and you'll be fine."

Viktor took in Kat's smart-ass expression and that special brand of American bravado that had attracted him from the moment he first laid eyes on her. She was the same woman. Scared, angry, about to give birth, but still the same woman he'd fallen for over drinks one weekend at the hotel bar where she worked.

A tremor stirred deep in his chest.

He'd chosen his role as Rasnovia's leader. Sure he'd been born to it, but he'd also embraced the duties involved from the time he was young. It had always been his life's purpose. His calling. And winning his country back, giving his people back their freedoms, bringing his country into democracy, it was a burden only he could shoulder.

A burden Kat had never asked to bear.

They were only after her because of him. Because of the baby she carried. He had to get her out of here, somewhere she could be safe.

Lora Leigh glanced at her watch. "How many minutes between contractions?"

Kat shook her head. "I'm not sure. Um, maybe between ten and fifteen?"

"All right. That's good. I think you should have plenty of time to get to a hospital. Things usually progress slowly for a first baby."

"I'm not sure we can go to a hospital."

All three turned to stare at Viktor. Lora Leigh spoke first. "Why not?"

"The men who are after Kat, they have ways of getting their hands on information. And after the shooting in the barn, I'm betting they'll use those resources to check hospitals, just in case she was hit."

"The hospital has security, and we can hire more."

Viktor trusted Flint, but he wasn't sure about security he didn't know. Once upon a time, he'd believed he could trust palace security. He'd been horribly wrong. "As much money and influence as the Rasnovian rebels seem to have backing them, I'm not sure we can trust anyone." He looked at Lora Leigh. She'd said she wasn't a doctor, but at this moment, she was as close to an expert on childbirth as he could get.

"I wouldn't condone trying to deliver this baby without a hospital. Kat jokes, but I really am a horse vet. I'm not qualified in the least to deliver a child. Kat is in great health, but that doesn't guarantee something won't go wrong."

"So I'll go to a hospital in Galveston instead. Or somewhere else. I'll check in under a false name." Kat watched him, waiting for his response.

"Do you have fake identification?" Viktor asked.

Kat shook her head and glanced at Lora Leigh. "Will they turn me away if I don't have ID?"

Lora Leigh tilted her head to the side. "I wouldn't think so. But the way the system is nowadays, I can't say for sure."

Dogs barked outside.

Viktor tensed. Wherever those dogs were, they hadn't noticed his and Kat's approach. What did they see or hear this time that caught their attention?

Flint strode to the foyer.

Kat nodded to Lora Leigh, as if the problem was solved. "If they ask me for ID, we'll figure out something else."

Like what? Viktor hadn't a clue. He watched Flint peer through one of the sidelight windows flanking the front door. "A deputy's here." A warning note sounded in his voice. A tone that matched the uneasy stretch of the muscles running up Viktor's spine.

Kat hefted herself up from the sofa. "That was quick."

"Yes. Too quick." Viktor thrust out a hand at Flint. He didn't have to tell his friend not to answer. Without a word passing between them, Flint reached to the side of the door and flicked off the foyer lights.

Viktor crossed into the darkened formal dining room at the front of the house. He pulled back a corner of the sheer drapes and peered out the window into the darkness.

It took a moment for his eyes to adjust. A glowing white gleam reflected off a sheriff's car parked in the circular drive.

Inside the house, footsteps approached on the hardwood floor. The unmistakable clacking of a shotgun chambering its cartridge sounded behind him. Flint cleared his throat. "What do you see?"

The driver's door opened. The overhead light revealed a single deputy inside. He climbed out. The man looked young, yet sported a blond high and tight and a hardness to his jaw that suggested former military. "There's one car. Only one deputy."

"Only one deputy called out for a shooting? Maybe more are on their way."

"If that's true, why isn't he waiting for the others?" Viktor tracked the man as he circled his car and started in the direction of the front door.

"Jackson had some trouble with a detective." Even from a distance, Viktor could hear the tremble in Lora Leigh's voice.

"The man was dirty as the day is long," Kat added. "Maybe he wasn't the only one."

Flint shifted his position, getting a better angle on the view outside. He grunted. "I know this guy. Bobby Lee Stubfield. Most of the deputies in this county are professional. Nice guys and gals. But this one? He's a real piece of work."

Something stirred the darkness beyond the

county squad car, beyond the deputy. Some kind of movement. More men. One? Two? They were dressed in dark clothing, not sheriff's uniforms, but something military in flavor.

He hoped Kat really was able to travel, because they bloody well couldn't stay. "Time to go."

Chapter Three

"You'd better hurry."

Kat had known Lora Leigh for several months now, and she could have sworn the woman was unflappable. No matter what situation she'd faced with the horses, the blond dynamo's hands were steady and her presence was soothing. Now, her voice trembled.

An answering tremble rippled up Kat's spine and seized her fingers, her hands, her arms. Despite the air-conditioning in the house, her maternity top stuck to her skin and sweat slicked her back. She wrapped her arms around her abdomen to stop the shaking.

It was all catching up to her. The men in the barn. Her close escape. Viktor back from the dead. The fact that her baby was on his way. She'd been struggling to process everything that had happened, to keep control of her emotions. Now the combustible mix of fear and anger and shock seemed to be working its way out through her fingertips, through her pores.

"We'll go to a hospital in Houston. You'll have to check in under another name."

She nodded. As long as more of those brutal men couldn't find her, she'd go to any hospital, she'd take any name he chose. "I just want to make sure the baby is okay."

"The baby will be fine. I promise."

Kat nodded. It was probably better if she pretended that was an outcome Viktor had control over.

"You'd better go out the back." Flint clapped a hand on Viktor's shoulder. "What do you want me to tell the deputy?"

Kat frowned. She couldn't have heard him right. "You have to come with us."

"Someone has got to stay, stall them. If no one answers the door, it's not going to take them long to figure out we saw through their charade."

"Those men...they're dangerous." Flint and Lora Leigh had been Kat's rocks over the last impossible months. The idea that they might be hurt in this, or killed...she couldn't bear it. She glanced up at Viktor. "They need to come with us."

Viktor narrowed his eyes on his friend. "Kat's right. These men don't care about the law."

"We've had trouble here before. I've taken steps to make sure it doesn't happen again. Or at least if it does, we're prepared." He lifted the shotgun as if offering proof.

Viktor nodded. But Kat couldn't let her concern go quite so easily. "What are you going to do? Take on a whole army with a single shotgun?"

Flint chuckled. "Remember those men I told you about? The ones I trust? I can have them here in thirty seconds. Mercenary soldiers or not, I can't see them starting a war on U.S. soil. Not when what they want is no longer here." Flint gave her shoulder a reassuring squeeze and turned his attention to Viktor. "Now we're wasting time. What should I tell him? I want to make sure we're all on the same page."

"Stick with your report that you heard gunfire and don't know who was responsible."

Nodding, Flint dipped a hand into his pocket and drew out a set of keys. He flipped them to Viktor with a jingle. "Look for a black pickup outside the stud barn. It should have a full tank."

"I owe you."

"The only thing you owe me is an explanation. And I'm going to hold you to that."

"Deal."

"We've got to stick together, Viktor. The Aggie Four. No matter what kind of resources those damn rebels have, we can beat them if we stick together. Don't shut us out this time."

Viktor nodded. "I'll contact you." He reached out and took Kat's hand, his tight grip stilling her fingers' trembling.

But the tremble deep inside didn't let up.

The last five months she'd believed she was in this alone. That everything was up to her. The fact that Viktor was here now didn't seem real. It hadn't fully sunk in. Maybe it would help if she knew what had happened to him. If she understood why he'd let her think he was dead. Why he hadn't trusted her. Maybe then she could make some kind of sense out of all this.

But no matter what her mind did or didn't grasp, her body knew his touch, accepted it, and responded.

They started down the hall to the back door.

"Take care of yourselves, you two." Lora Leigh's voice followed them. "Yourselves and your little prince."

IT WASN'T UNTIL they'd located Flint's pickup, driven the back way off the ranch land and reached the highway that Kat could organize her mind enough to ask. But just as the most current contraction faded and her mouth was ready to form the words, Viktor turned to her with a question of his own. "Flint's wife said, 'Take care of your little prince.'"

She was wondering if he'd picked that up. "I had an ultrasound. We're having a boy."

He pressed his lips together. A weak attempt at a smile. The green tinge of the dashboard lights accentuated worry lines digging into his forehead.

"I thought you'd be happy."

"I am."

"What is it, then?"

"Nothing."

As if she bought that. "Bull."

He blew out a resigned breath. "If it was a girl, I'd hoped the rebels might not feel so threatened. Wishful thinking. It probably wouldn't matter either way."

The tone of his voice was flat. Borderline hopeless. She'd never heard him sound like that when talking about any problem his country faced. It frightened her to hear him sound like that now. "What happened to you in Rasnovia? Why did you let us all believe you were dead?"

For a long time, he didn't answer. He just stared at the straight ribbon of highway stretching ahead. Tires hummed over pavement. On the radio, Dale Watson sang a country ballad asking whether he was blessed or damned. She was about to repeat her question when Viktor finally spoke. "I don't remember much about the explosion. Not what happened before. Not what happened after."

She remembered the parts before and after all too well. She'd flown to Rasnovia right before the country's independence celebration to break the news of her pregnancy to Viktor. But she'd been miles away from the main palace when the bomb exploded, safely tucked away in the royal family's chalet in the northern Rasnovian mountains. Instead of being by Viktor's side, she'd watched the ceremony on television, worried the appearance of the prince's pregnant American girlfriend would send shockwaves of scandal through the country. A half hour into the celebration, that became the most trivial of her concerns.

"The only thing I really do remember was the smell. Blood. Burning flesh. Dust that clogged my throat like paste. My first clear memory was waking up in Ilona Vargha's home."

"I don't know the name."

"She worked at the palace. My mother's personal secretary. She told me about the bomb. She said my mother was dead. My sister, too. Two aunts, an uncle, cousins…everyone."

A sharp pain moved through Kat's sinuses. Tears pooled in her eyes. It wasn't fair. None of it. Viktor's father had been assassinated when he was a teen growing up in London. And now the rest of his family? It was too cruel to be believed.

She swiped at her eyes with the back of a hand. "I'm so sorry."

He nodded his thanks.

She knew it wasn't enough, but she didn't know what else to say. She had no way of understanding what he'd been through, how he felt now.

Her life had been easy. Upper middle class parents. A childhood in the Chicago suburbs. No one to worry about but herself. Before these last few months, the hardest thing she'd ever done was serve lumberjack breakfasts to conventioneers at a resort in Wisconsin. Her career in restaurant management had been stressful on occasion, but she couldn't pretend dealing with an irrate guest's overdone steak was a life-and-death situation. She made okay money. She'd done what she wanted, when she wanted. Until she'd become pregnant, she hadn't understood what it was like to live for anyone other than herself.

"If it wasn't for Ilona and her family, I wouldn't be here. She risked everything."

"How long were you unconscious?"

He grimaced, as if reliving unpleasant memories. "A day. Maybe a little more. I called Akeem as soon as I could."

"Why Akeem? Why not the others in The Aggie Four? Why not me?"

"Akeem was in the Middle East at the time. He was close."

"I was in Rasnovia."

He glanced at her with troubled eyes. "You have

to understand. Akeem has contacts you don't have. In Rasnovia. In the surrounding countries. In Mexico. I knew he could get you back to America. He could make sure you were safe."

And he had. A fact for which she'd always be grateful. But that wasn't the point she'd been trying to make. "Why did you let me believe you were dead?"

"What would you have done if you'd known the truth?"

What would she do? She couldn't say. It had been a frightening time. The explosion. The rebels taking over the government. Fighting in the streets. She was just a girl from the suburbs. Naive and clueless. But she liked to think she would have stepped up when the chips were down. Done something that mattered. Even if she didn't have the first idea of what that would have been. Really, for her, it all came down to one thing. "At least I could have been there for you."

"Exactly why I didn't want you to know."

His words stung like a slap across the cheek. "You didn't want—"

He glanced at her, then into the rearview mirror. Lines pressed around his eyes and at the corners of his mouth. "If you had stayed in Rasnovia, how long do you think it would have taken for the rebels to find you? To learn who you were? To figure out exactly why you were visiting the country in the first place?"

She moved her arms lower, hugging her belly and the baby inside.

Again, he tore his eyes from the road and glanced at her. His gaze shifted low. "That's why."

She forced her arms to her side. "If you'd explained that my being there endangered the baby, I would have listened. I would have left."

"Would you? Even if you believed I wouldn't live out the week? Because that's what Ilona thought. That's what everyone thought, even me. Would you have left if you believed I was dying? Or would you have insisted on staying for what little time I had left?"

She couldn't answer. Not without conceding his point.

"Kat," he said, his voice suddenly soft. "Americans don't really understand how to blend in. If you had stayed, you would have been discovered."

She opened her mouth to defend herself, but shut it without uttering a word. He was right about that, too. She didn't know the language. She didn't know the customs. All she'd known about Rasnovia were the stories Viktor had told her during his visits to the U.S. and what little scenery she'd taken in on her chauffeured ride from the airport the day before. As much as she liked to dream about what a heroine she would have been, it was only a fantasy. The product of watching too many Hollywood movies where the brave American rode to the rescue. The average person overcame the odds. "So you could have explained those things to me. I'm not stupid. I wouldn't have put you or the baby at risk."

"Kat, that's the point. I wasn't in shape to explain anything."

She let out a sigh and wiped her cheeks once again. What he said made sense. Every bit of it. Flint and Jackson would have insisted on helping, too, had they known Viktor survived. They had done much more traveling than she had, but they both had a larger-than-life way about them that didn't blend in well anywhere but in Texas. For all she knew, they were well-known in Rasnovia, both having done a lot of business there with The Aggie Four Foundation. She could understand all the points Viktor had made about his decision.

Then why couldn't she accept it?

Her back began to tighten, and she leaned forward, all her concentration on breathing, riding the wave of pain instead of letting it drag her under. Seconds stretched, passing as slowly as minutes.

Viktor took a hand from the wheel and stroked her back. Up and down. Up and down. In rhythm with her breath.

Kat knew the pressure of his hand didn't really have a physical effect on her cramping muscles, but somehow she felt better all the same.

And that was what was wrong.

Bit by bit, the contraction released her. Her breath came easier. Her body returned to her control. Viktor withdrew his hand, and she leaned back in her seat, readjusting the safety belt over her shoulder.

Outside the truck, the fence lines and fields thinned and fell away. Housing developments, fast-food restaurants and big box stores took their place, developments more dense with each mile spinning under the tires. Up ahead, the lights of the city glowed in the night sky like a premature sunrise.

She cleared her throat and tried to push away the nervous jiggle that was seated low in her stomach. Viktor had said his piece. He'd explained what had happened to him, why he'd made the decisions he had. Now it was her turn.

She just hoped she could find the words.

"Viktor?"

She could feel his eyes flick in her direction, then return to the road.

"That night we were together in Rasnovia, when I told you about the baby, you asked me to marry you."

His chin lowered in an almost imperceptible nod.

Warmth flushed over her. She'd told him she didn't want to rush into marriage. That she wanted to make sure their love was real. After the explosion, she'd regretted her hesitation. She'd wished with all her heart that she'd thrown her arms around his neck and promised to love him forever. She'd been plagued by nightmares of him reaching out to her, injured and pleading, and her pushing him away.

But even though she'd replayed that question in her mind for months, until this minute, she hadn't known what her answer had to be. Until this moment, it hadn't been clear. "Ever since I was a little girl, I wanted a family of my own. A whole family, not one like mine where the mommy and daddy lived apart. I wanted to find a man I loved and become his wife. I suppose a lot of girls do. But it wasn't just playing dolls for me. Or dreaming of diamond rings and wedding dresses." It was hard admitting her feelings. Harder than she'd anticipated.

He made a low sound in his throat, letting her know he was listening, encouraging her to go on.

"To me, marriage is a partnership. The foundation for a family. Two people working together to build something bigger than themselves. That's what my parents never had. That's what I've always wanted. That's what I've always dreamed about." She paused again, afraid of what she needed to say next.

A muscle along Viktor's jaw hardened, then released. Headlights from behind reflected off the rearview mirror and highlighted lines of worry bracketing his eyes. "But?"

She let out a heavy breath. She needed to be honest with him. No matter how much it hurt, she had to say the rest. "You and I...we're not partners, Viktor."

He nodded, as if mulling that over. "We can become partners."

"Can we? I don't see how. Not when you refuse to let me in."

"How am I doing that?"

"By keeping the truth from me. By asking Akeem to whisk me away instead of leveling with me and deciding our future together. By not trusting me."

"By wanting to protect you?" He shook his head. "I've explained why I did what I did. And I'm not going to apologize for it."

"I know. And that's the problem." Tears filled her eyes again, turning the truck's interior into a wavy watercolor of green light and shadow. "I realized it when you were rubbing my back, helping me get through that last contraction."

"Realized what?"

"That you want to help me, protect me, take care of me, but you won't let me do the same for you."

"That's not true."

"Really? In all the time we spent together, have you let me handle one thing?"

"Handle? What do you mean?"

What did she mean? She needed an example, something concrete to help him understand. Her mind scrambled for an answer. "I don't know, like have you ever let me pay for anything?"

"I have a lot more money than you do, Kat."

"Make hotel arrangements? Book flights?" Her examples were lame, she knew. She was doing a horrible job of explaining what she meant. But she couldn't find anything else concrete to hold on to.

"I have a schedule I have to adhere to, a staff that did those things for me." He gripped the steering wheel and pressed his lips into a line. "You're about to have our baby. We have a mercenary army trying to kill us. I can't believe we're even having this conversation."

"I know it seems petty. Like nothing compared to all you've been through, all we face now. And I know I'm going about this all wrong. But I...I don't know how else to tell you how I feel."

He removed one hand from the wheel and enfolded her fingers in his. "If this situation ever ends, you can buy all the dinners and book all the flights you want."

A weight settled into her chest. She blinked back tears and stared through the windshield at the glow of Houston's lights ahead. He didn't get it. Not at all. And she had no clue how to change that. All she knew was that she wanted more. To be more. For Viktor. For her son. For herself.

She just prayed they all lived long enough for her to make that happen.

VIKTOR HADN'T KEPT TRACK of when Kat had her most recent contraction, but by the time they finally reached Houston's Southwest General Hospital, he'd have sworn the cramps had gotten closer together. And stronger.

It had taken every ounce of his willpower to stay in the truck and let her waddle into the emergency room on her own. If he'd gone with her, the hospital would no doubt have made him fill out paperwork, show identification or proof of insurance. And although Flint provided all his employees with health insurance, Kat couldn't tap into that without giving the hospital her name. So instead of Kat Edwards, Sue Anderson had checked into the hospital, according to plan. But instead of going ahead with his part of the plan— checking into a pit of a motel whose neon sign he could see from the truck—he sat in the parking lot outside the emergency room entrance and waited, for what, he wasn't sure.

The conversation they'd had earlier buzzed through Viktor's mind. When Kat had told him she was pregnant all those months ago in Rasnovia, he'd proposed out of more than duty. He was in love with her. He had no doubt about that. But while he was hurt by her refusal, he had to admit he was also relieved.

So much had happened since that cold night before his country's independence celebration. So much had changed. Back then he'd believed they could have a life together. That he and Kat and the baby could form a happy family. Now he understood that if Kat married him, she would only become even more of a target.

He checked his watch for the fiftieth time. Two hours had passed. For all he knew she could have had the baby by now.

Without him.

He slammed his palms on the steering wheel. The force shuddered up his arms. He hated this. Not being there. Not knowing what was happening. Not being able to control a bloody thing.

At least once the baby was born, he could get Kat out of Texas. He could hide her away in a place where no one knew her. Somewhere with no ties to him. Somewhere she and the baby wouldn't be harmed by the fight into which he'd been thrust.

Safe.

A throb of red light flashed off the truck's dashboard. He twisted in his seat. Behind him, an ambulance turned off the street and rushed up to one of the emergency bays. At least this place was busy enough that Kat could blend in. She was just another woman having a baby. And if all went well, if she and the baby were okay, he could sneak her out in a day or so without anyone realizing who she was.

Wait.

Peering past the ambulance, he focused on the white sheriff's squad car pulling into one of the slots reserved for police vehicles. When choosing a hospital, they'd opted for one on the opposite side of Houston from the ranch. This was a different county, and if Viktor remembered correctly, the sheriff in this county had different colored cars.

The squad car's door opened and a deputy climbed out. The man's head shone pink in the parking lot lights. At this distance, Viktor couldn't tell if he was bald or had very short, blond hair.

Viktor clamped his teeth together, hard. Had Deputy Stubfield followed them from the ranch? He'd been careful. But he'd also been distracted by Kat. Could he have missed a vehicle tailing them? Could he have bungled this whole thing?

The deputy circled his car, but instead of entering the emergency room, he walked back to the street. He stepped up to a dark sedan idling at the curb. The tinted passenger window lowered, and Viktor could see at least two men inside.

There was only one reason these men were lingering outside a busy hospital in Houston. Either they'd been followed, or someone in the hospital had, for some reason, reported Kat's presence to the police.

Viktor had to get Kat out of there, and he needed to do it quickly and quietly.

He eyed the emergency room entrance. If this hospital was like so many others in big cities all across America, it had a metal detector at the door. He wouldn't be able to bring his pistol. Not that he planned to have a shootout with a lawman in the hospital halls, but the thought of being unarmed wasn't a pleasant one. He unbuckled his holster and stuffed it and the weapon under the truck seat. He'd have to find another way to bring a weapon inside.

He scanned the pickup's king cab. A jumble of boxes filled the backseat. A toolbox, two hat boxes and one that looked like it might contain boots. The toolbox yielded a small pair of scissors, which he stuffed in a back pocket. Not much of a weapon, but at least if it set off an alarm, he would be able to pass it off as an innocent mistake. He opened one of the hat boxes. Inside lay a straw Resistol, crown down to keep its shape. He lifted it from the box and fit it on his head. A little tight, but it would do.

Inside the boot box he found a pair of ostrich Tony Lamas. Nice. He and Flint wore the same size back in college days. Back then, Flint was scrambling for money and used to borrow Viktor's Italian-made loafers whenever he had to attend an event where beat up, manure-kicking Ropers weren't appropriate attire. He slipped off his shoes and pulled on the boots. Apparently Flint's shoe size hadn't changed.

He pulled the legs of his black trousers over the boot shafts. It would be better if he was wearing jeans, but he didn't have much choice there. He'd have to take his chances that the hat and boots were enough.

And that neither the deputy nor the mercenaries would have their eyes out for a dead man.

Chapter Four

Viktor stepped to the registration desk in the hospital emergency room. If there was one thing he'd learned in the years he'd spent attending universities and making connections all over the world, it was that people from each area shared certain mannerisms that made them fit into their specific cultural surroundings. Clothing, of course. Accents. But also posture, length of stride, hand gestures, eye contact.

As luck would have it, he'd spent a lot of time in Texas, so much that the mates he'd grown up with in London likely wouldn't recognize him for all the Texas-flavored verbal mannerisms and body language he'd adopted as his own. And his lifelong friendships gave him even more insight when it came to passing for a native Texan. If he wanted to glide by as a Houston businessman, he needed only to channel Jackson Champion and Deke Norton. If he wanted to blend in as a cowboy, he had only to exaggerate the mannerisms he'd picked up from Flint McKade.

He tilted his hat back on his forehead the way he'd seen Flint do a thousand times. Cocking a hip, he leaned against the high desk and gave the nurse a purely Texas smile. "Pardon, ma'am. I'm looking for my wife."

The nurse peered up at him and then back at the computer screen in front of her. Judging from the redness of her eyes and the lines digging between her brows and bracketing her mouth, she was near the end of a very long shift. She looked exhausted enough to lay her head down and pass out on her keyboard at any moment. "Name?"

Out of the corner of his eye, he spotted the dark blue county uniform coming through the emergency room entrance. He tilted his head, shielding his face with the hat brim. "Name's Sue Anderson."

The nurse stared at her computer and frowned, as if she'd forgotten how to read the thing.

The deputy strode past him without a second look and waved down a nurse.

The nurse looking for Kat didn't move. Didn't blink. At this rate, by the time she found Kat's fake name, Kat herself would already be in Deputy Stubfield's custody.

Viktor hooked his thumbs in the front pockets of his trousers so he wouldn't strangle the poor woman out of sheer frustration. "Sue Anderson? She's having a baby," he prompted.

"Oh, then you want the maternity floor. But first, I see Susan Anderson wasn't able to fill out her insurance paperwork. So if we could get that handled…" She pushed a clipboard at him.

The nurse helping the deputy sat down at a computer terminal and started efficiently punching keys.

Just his luck. He'd chosen the wrong line. Or maybe it was just the uniform that inspired competence and speed in the overworked hospital staff. He took the clipboard from the nurse helping him. "If I can trouble you further, where is the maternity ward?"

She didn't even look up at him. "It's on another floor. I'll have someone direct you once you've filled out that paperwork."

"Thanks so much." He tried his best to bite back his sarcasm, but he wasn't sure if he succeeded. So much for that idea. By the time he received official directions to Kat's room, it would be too late. He'd already lost his head start in the time he'd wasted trying to secure directions. He and Deputy Stubfield would likely reach Kat's room at nearly the same time. He couldn't afford to piss around for another second.

He took the clipboard and stepped away from

the desk. Spotting a restroom on the edge of the waiting area, he walked toward it, trying to affect the relaxed, ambling gate Flint and so many other Texas cowboys were so good at. He ducked into the restroom and dropped the clipboard into the trash can along with his hat. Too bad. It was a nice hat. He'd have to buy Flint another.

He turned on the tap, dipped his hands and raked wet fingers through his hair, slicking it back from his face. Unrolling the sleeves of his button-down shirt, he smoothed down the wrinkles and peered into the mirror. Instead of a cowboy, a casual young professional peered back at him. It would be nice to add a tie or jacket to really change his look, but this would have to do. With any luck all the deputy and hospital personnel had really noticed was the hat, the drawl, the ambling gait of a cowboy.

Now to find the maternity floor.

He strode from the bathroom and turned away from the emergency room, following a long, wide hall which according to signs, led to a cafeteria and gift shop. A bouquet of flowers might be a nice touch to allow him to blend in with the other husbands bringing gifts to their wives after the birth of their babies, but at this hour, the flower shop was closed. Instead, he stopped at a vending machine and bought a cup of watery, horrid-smelling brew and made for the closest lift.

Elevator, he corrected himself. He had to remember that. In the years he'd lived in America, he'd shed most of his British-isms, but he still slid into his old ways once in a while. Elevator. No American would call it a lift.

He found a small hall punctuated with six doors and punched the up button. Craning his neck, he studied the floor directory posted over the doors. Not one, but three floors were devoted to maternity. How he would know which one Kat was on, he hadn't a clue. A bell chimed, a door slid open, and he stepped inside.

A blue uniform flashed in his peripheral vision. He turned around just as the sheriff's deputy stepped into the lif…elevator. The man looked at him with sharp brown eyes.

Viktor returned his gaze, forcing himself to keep his breathing steady despite the fact that his heart felt like it was about to beat out of his chest. He could feel the small scissors in his back pocket. What a joke. If the deputy recognized him, this charade would be over in a blink. No gun would save him, unless he was willing to commit cold-blooded murder. A tiny pair of scissors was as good as nothing.

He gave the lawman what he hoped was a casual nod. Averting his face, he gestured to the numbered buttons in front of him. "Floor?"

"Fifteen. Thanks."

Viktor pushed the button. Was Kat on the fifteenth floor? Had the deputy figured out the false name she'd given the hospital? He had no way of knowing, but he couldn't take the chance. Keeping his face turned to the side, he pretended to indulge in the tradition of watching the lighted numbers above the door. "Wife having a baby?"

"No."

"I hope you're not here on business." He sneaked a look in Deputy Stubfield's direction.

The deputy was staring at the lighted numbers, as well. "Actually, I am."

Viktor's shoulders slumped slightly with relief. Apparently Stubfield wasn't much for chatting. Fine with Viktor. Too much talking and the hint of the British accent he still carried might come through. And the deputy hadn't seemed to recognized Viktor, either. Not surprising. Americans liked to focus on themselves, not the rest of the world. The average man on the street didn't know the name of the United States Secretary of Defense. He sure didn't know the face of a prince of an obscure country in Eastern Europe. And, luckily for Viktor, apparently neither did the average deputy.

Now if he didn't know what Kat looked like, either, maybe Viktor still had a chance of reaching her first.

The upward motion slowed and braked to a halt. Chime sounding, the door slid open. Viktor held back, letting the deputy exit first. He turned to the right, heading for the nurse's desk. And to Viktor's relief, there wasn't a nurse in sight.

Viktor veered right. From the look of the halls, there were at least two long halls with rooms on either side. With a hospital tower this big, that made for a lot of rooms. If he wanted to find Kat before a nurse ushered the deputy to her room, he'd better hurry.

"YOU'RE ONLY AT FIVE CENTIMETERS."

Kat pulled her feet from the stirrups and smoothed her flimsy cotton hospital gown over her thighs. The contractions were getting stronger and closer together. She'd hoped all of this would be over soon. "That means I'm halfway there?"

"Yes." The nurse practitioner gave her a world-weary smile. "But none of this is an exact science. Your body might be ready in an hour or twelve, I really can't say."

"Let's make it an hour."

The woman's smile widened automatically, as if every patient she'd ever had made that same quip.

Kat groaned inwardly. She wasn't even original anymore. Maybe that's what happened when people were trying to kill you. Your sense of humor was wiped away right along with your sense of safety and well-being.

She'd have to ask Viktor.

She still couldn't wrap her mind around the fact that he was alive. It had taken months for her to accept that he'd been killed in that palace explosion. Weeks of crying followed by months where she didn't feel anything at all. Now having him back, and learning that he'd chosen not to tell her he was still alive...she didn't know what she felt. Anger, at first, but even that was already dissipating. Beyond that? She hadn't a clue.

Her back began to tighten. She braced herself for the contraction. It wrapped around her, claiming her back, belly, legs.

Her whole body.

She panted hard. Lying on her back like this was the worst. She felt so out of control. So open to the tightening cramp. She preferred to hunch forward, move in the direction of the contraction. But she could get through it. It wouldn't last. She had to remember that, to focus on that. She could handle the pain. It would be over soon.

"Sue."

Something shifted inside her at the sound of his voice. Warmth flowed over her. In the back of her mind, she knew it meant something had gone wrong. She knew he'd have to be desperate to veer from their plan. Yet knowing all that, she couldn't help the comfort, the relief at the thought that he was here. That she wasn't all alone anymore. She held up a hand, breathing far too hard to get her voice to function.

The nurse looked up from her equipment. "Can I help you?"

"I'm the baby's father. May we have a moment alone?"

The nurse glanced Kat's way.

Bit by bit the contraction eased. But she still couldn't find her voice. Kat nodded, hoping that would suffice.

Luckily, a nod and a busy schedule will get an overworked nurse out of a room. Fast.

As she cleared the door, Viktor stepped to the side of the bed and grasped Kat's hand. "We have to go. Now."

The cramp pulled back. Slowly. As her mind cleared, she focused on Viktor. Muscles strained along his jaw. Tight lines rimmed the outer edge of his eyes.

The sense of well-being his presence had given her crumbled, giving way to the fear coursing underneath. "What…what happened?"

Viktor's eyes darted around the room. "Your clothes. Where are they? We have to get out of here."

That could only mean one thing. "They're coming?"

"Deputy Stubfield is at the nurses' station. At least two men are in the parking lot."

Kat released the railing on the right of the narrow hospital bed and draped her legs over the side. With Viktor's help, she heaved herself to her feet. Her clothes. She pointed to the set of closets on one side of the tiny room. "My jeans and shirt are in there."

Viktor gathered her clothes.

She pulled off her hospital gown. Before she'd gotten pregnant, she used to be embarrassed when it came to showing her body. After endless prenatal exams complete with strangers poking and prodding her in the most intimate areas, she no longer thought of her body as anything worth being modest about. Her breasts surged huge and full, as big and round as the silicone attributes of a stripper. Her skin stretched taut over her swollen belly. She couldn't even see anything below that.

Viktor turned around, holding her stretch-belly jeans and tent-like top. His gaze rested on her breasts. But although her body had changed so much since the last time he'd seen it, his expression didn't. He looked at her with all the desire he had when her belly was flat and her breasts perky. Maybe more. "Uh, here." He handed her the clothes, but he didn't look away.

Warmth tingled over her skin. Emotion tightened her throat, feelings she didn't have time to feel—now or ever.

Skipping the bra and panties, she dragged on her clothes as quickly as she could while Viktor peeked into the hall. "It's clear. But I hear voices. Hurry."

Finished dressing, she stepped up behind him. He reached back for her and took her hand in his. They scurried out into the hall.

Out here, she could hear the voices, too. The nurse who had checked her progress and the deeper tone of a man's voice. They were heading this way.

"In here." Viktor pushed a door open and ducked inside. He pulled Kat in after.

She crowded in next to him, her side pressing against what felt like a steel rack. The scent of cleaning supplies stung her sinuses and made her feel sick to her stomach.

"We'll wait for them to clear out and find a stairwell."

"I noticed one when they had me walking earlier. It's halfway down the hall on this side. Turn right."

"Good."

"But we're on the fifteenth floor." She was having contractions every five minutes. At that rate, it would take them forever to reach the lobby.

"We just need to go down one floor or two. Then we can cross to an elevator."

It sounded easy. She wanted to believe it would be.

The nurse's alarmed voice filtered through the door followed by the male voice barking orders. Their voices grew louder, as if they were right outside the storage closet.

Kat's pulse pounded in her ears. She pressed a hand to her chest, as if she could quiet the beat. Any second she expected the closet door to open and the deputy to be peering down at them, gun in his fist. One second passed. Two.

The voices faded.

"Now." Viktor pushed the door open. He peeked into the hall and then pulled her out behind him. "Run."

Kat tried her best to keep up with a fast waddle. Using her free hand, she cupped her arm under her belly, trying to relieve the weight on tired muscles. As long as the contraction held off long enough for them to find a stairwell, she could keep up.

They rounded the corner and hurried down the next hall. Voices jangled behind them. Viktor glanced back at her as if willing her to move faster.

Her breathing rasped in her ears. God, she hoped she was right about the location of the stairwell. She had to be. She scanned the hall ahead, searching for the exit sign. There it was. Halfway down the hall. She gritted her teeth and forced her legs to keep moving. Deep in her lower back, she felt the muscles starting to tighten.

Twenty feet to the exit door. She plowed on, Viktor half pulling her. The cramp spread around her sides and across her lower abdomen. Ten feet. The voices were louder, plenty loud, yet somehow she couldn't make out a word they were saying. Were they real? Or where they just in her mind? She couldn't tell. She couldn't think. She focused on her feet slapping the tile, the squeeze of Viktor's hand.

He yanked open the stairwell door. He scooped his arm around her back, ushering her inside. The door clanked shut behind them.

Kat lurched forward, bracing her hands on her knees. The pain crescendoed to full volume, blocking out her senses, blotting out all thought. All she could focus on, all she could feel was that relentless pain wrapping around her, threading through her, squeezing her like a giant fist.

She wasn't sure how long the contraction lasted. It seemed longer than the rest. An eternity. And even though she half expected someone to burst through the door at any moment, if it happened she knew there wasn't a thing she could do.

Finally the pain started to retreat, pulling back like the tide. Her mind cleared. The dank smell of cold concrete and dust filled her senses. The heavy sound of her breathing echoed off the walls. Still hunched forward, she peered up at Viktor. "I'm ready. Let's go."

"Are you sure?"

"I have less than five minutes until the next one. We'd better hurry."

He nodded. Still gripping her hand, he led the way down the steps. He passed the next floor landing and descended another flight before reaching for the door handle. He pulled the door open and peered into the hall. "All clear. Go."

Kat scurried out after him. The layout of this floor was exactly like the one above, except instead of a hallway decorated in light mauve and baby blue, this was sterile shades of gray. She glanced through an open door. An older man sat upright in his bed, watching television. He didn't seem to notice them pass. The loud jingle of a commercial followed them down the hall.

They reached a bank of elevators. Climbing aboard one of the cars, they took it down to the lobby. As the elevator slowed, she glanced up at Viktor. She still couldn't believe he was here. But the fact that she was about to give birth to his baby had become very real to her in the past few hours. And more than anything, she wanted to get somewhere safe before it happened. "How close is the next hospital?"

"I don't know. Not too far. There are a lot of hospitals in the Houston area. Only—"

"Only what?"

"I'm not sure we can get to the pickup. The men who came with Stubfield, they're parked nearby. They didn't recognize me going in, but if I come out with you, they're bound to notice."

"What do we do?"

"Find another vehicle? Steal one?"

He didn't sound very sure of that plan. "Do you know how to do that?"

"I'll figure it out."

She shook her head. Sneaking from a hospital in the middle of labor. Stealing cars. This was crazy.

The elevator slowed its descent.

She shifted her feet. Wetness soaked into her jeans. A drop trickled down her inner thigh, tickling a track to her knee before it soaked into denim. She shifted again. Had she wet her pants? No. She knew what it was. "My water just broke."

"The baby is coming? Now?"

"Not right this minute." She shook her head. It seemed nothing in this birth business happened *that* quickly. She was beginning to think the whole thing was a particularly cruel type of slow torture. "He'll be here soon, though."

The elevator door slid open. Kat half expected the deputy or brutal-looking soldiers like the ones in the horse barn would be standing there, waiting for them. But the hall was empty.

They wound their way through corridors and out the first exit they found. Although the night was warm, the air felt deliciously cool on her skin. Not only were her jeans dark with wetness, but her maternity top stuck to her sweaty back like plastic wrap.

Viktor pointed to a side street leading away from the glaring lights of the hospital entrance. "There are some cars parked down there."

Kat tried to imagine Viktor breaking into a car, finding a way to start it without a key, stealing it from some unsuspecting owner. She couldn't see it. Not for a second. And if they succeeded? Where would they go then? "Forget it."

"We have to do something. We can't stay here."

"And if we go to another hospital, can you say they won't find us there?"

He shook his head. "I don't know if someone tipped them off or if we were followed from the ranch. All I know is we can't stay here."

"How about the motel? The one you were going to stay in while I was in the hospital?"

Viktor opened his mouth, then closed it as if he had no clue what to say.

"It's close, right?"

"Yes."

"Close enough so that if anything goes wrong, or if the baby is in trouble, we can call the hospital?"

"Kat, who's going to deliver the baby? I've already tried calling Flint and Lora Leigh, and there's no answer."

Worry washed over her like a wave. She prayed Flint and Lora Leigh were all right. She wished more than anything they had come with her and Viktor. Not only would she know they were safe now, but Lora Leigh would be here to deliver her baby. She might have only delivered foals, but at least it was something. "You. You can deliver him."

Viktor's eyes widened, as if he'd never considered the possibility until now and it scared the hell straight out of him. "I don't know, Kat. I—"

"Have always taken care of me and protected me. And you can do it again now."

Chapter Five

The motel was a seedy dump. The kind of place barely a half step up from those that rent rooms by the hour to ladies of the night. Not a place in which Viktor had thought he'd ever stay, let alone bring his first child into the world.

At least the front desk took cash and asked no questions.

He pulled the old-fashioned metal key attached to a plastic paddle from his pocket and slipped it into the lock. His hands were surprisingly steady, yet it still took three tries before he lined the key up well enough to slide it home. The knob turned easily under his hand, and he pushed the door open.

The room was small enough to size up with a single glance. Candy colors of blue and green decorated the single queen-sized bed and blended with green carpet and blue wallpaper. Prints that appeared as though the local school kids had slapped them together decorated the walls. The lingering stench of stale cigarette smoke and mildew hung in the air, heavy as the humidity of an approaching thunderstorm.

Kat trudged past him and lowered herself to the edge of the bed. "It's not so bad."

Sure. It would be fine. As long as nothing went wrong. He closed the door. "I doubt they'll be looking for us here, at any rate."

He threw the deadbolt and secured the flimsy chain. They should be safe here. At least for a while. He passed a bathroom the size of a small linen closet and set the large plastic bag he was carrying on a press-board dresser. They'd stopped at a drug store on their walk from the hospital and picked up food and whatever supplies they could possibly imagine needing, including plastic and towels to contain the inevitable blood and birth fluids. After smelling this room, he wondered why he ever thought protecting the mattress was necessary. More important was protecting Kat and the baby from lurking germs.

What the hell was he doing?

He'd trained all his life to be a diplomat and an economist. He was no doctor. He had no business delivering the baby. If something went wrong…

Kat groaned. She perched on the edge of the bed, leaning forward, her arms around her middle.

Viktor had never been one to focus on doubt

instead of taking action, and he couldn't afford to do that now. He had to be there for Kat. Nothing would go wrong. He couldn't let it.

"Hold on." He climbed onto the bed behind her and positioned himself so she was leaning back against his chest. He wrapped his arms around her as the pain took a hard hold. "Breathe, baby. I'm here. You're doing fine. Just breathe."

Kat hunched forward against his arms. Her chest rose and fell as she breathed. In and out. In and out.

He wasn't sure how long they sat like that, riding through contraction after contraction together. In between, he kneaded the tight muscles in her shoulders and rubbed her temples with gentle fingers. Soaking in her scent and her softness, he planted a kiss on the rose tattooed on the nape of her neck and remembered the nights they'd shared, the laughs, the good times, all so very far away now. At one point, he got up and gathered towels, washed the scissors in his pocket with scalding water, and did whatever he could think of to be ready for the baby's eventual appearance. The in-betweens became shorter and shorter until they barely qualified as a short pause before the next contraction.

Kat hung in there as one hour stretched into the next. She was stronger than Viktor had ever guessed she could be, riding with the pressure, bracing for the next wave. He wished he could take the pain for her. Protect her from it. But he couldn't. All he could do was be there for her. Comfort her. Do little things to help.

"I have to push…I have to—" A grunt of pain cut off Kat's words. Then another. The sound was low and guttural, emanating from deep inside. Tears streamed down her cheeks and dripped from her chin.

He remembered his mantra. "Breathe. Remember to breathe."

She panted. Finally her breathing slowed as the contraction let up. For a moment, she looked at him with clear eyes. "He's coming."

He glanced at her bare legs. "Can you feel him?"

"Sort of. Not really. It's the pressure. I just know." Her face tensed. Again a groan built deep in her chest.

He squeezed her hand. He forced himself to release her fingers and slip out from behind her. He piled pillows to brace her back and moved to the bottom of the bed.

The scent of blood suffused his senses and coated the back of his throat. Coppery, fleshy and warm. His first look between her splayed legs made him shudder. Blood coated her thighs and leaked into the sheets. And in the middle, a huge mass of blood— Wait. Not blood. A head.

His baby's head. "I see him."

Kat's whole body heaved. Something between a scream and a moan erupted from her lips.

Viktor grasped one of the stack of clean towels he'd tossed at the base of the bed. He unfolded it so it would be ready. He reached out his hands for the little guy, then pulled them back. If he touched the baby, would he hurt him? Would he hurt Kat? He didn't know what to do.

Kat pushed again, and the head poked out farther. Black hair covered the crown. Little eyes, a nose, a mouth faced down, into the bed. He was so dark red, he was almost purple.

Again, Kat's muscles slackened. She peered at him from between her knees. "You can see him?"

"His head. It's out."

"I read that sometimes their shoulders get stuck. If that happens, can you pull him?" Her lips pulled back. She grimaced with pain.

There was almost no time between contractions now. No time for Kat to even catch her breath.

"I have him. I have him. Don't worry. Just push."

Kat gritted her teeth, the sound coming from her throat more a growl than a scream now.

Viktor fitted his fingers around the little guy's head, probing deep for his shoulders. He felt the tiny bones, the solid flesh. He tried to gently jimmy him free.

"Come on, little guy. Come on."

A surge of heat engulfed his hands. And then the baby was suddenly there, all bloody and purple. A slimy mass.

Viktor grabbed for the towel. He wrapped it around the little body. He took out the scissors and he cut the umbilical cord connecting baby to mother. The baby lay on the bed, his still little body dark against the white terrycloth. Unmoving.

Viktor's lungs constricted. Something was wrong. He remembered stories about doctors slapping babies, getting them to breathe. But he didn't think that was right. An old wives' tale. Slapping something that tiny and vulnerable could only cause damage.

"How is he?" Kat struggled to sit up higher, strained to see.

Viktor wiped the baby's nose and mouth gently, trying to clear them. He moved his hands under the little body, under the towel. The baby's tiny muscles seized.

Oh, God.

He looked up at Kat for a moment, mouth open. Was something wrong? He wanted to tell her, to ask, but he couldn't find the words.

The baby moved again. The little mouth opened. A cry erupted. Strangled at first, then gaining strength, volume. Mewing fast as a frightened kitten.

"Thank God," Kat whispered. A fresh surge of tears glistened on her cheeks.

Viktor closed his mouth. He looked down at his crying son. God, he was little. So little. Viktor's hand was as big as the baby's whole head.

"Can I see him?"

He started to lift the baby from the bed, the towel wrapping him stained red. His hands were awkward. So big and clumsy. He couldn't shake the feeling that if he didn't place his hands perfectly, he'd hurt the baby. He could probably hurt him with a misaimed glance.

A weight bore down on his chest, making it hard for his heart to keep its beat. Ever since he'd learned the rebels had discovered Kat's whereabouts, he'd lived with the overwhelming fear that she would be hurt. Killed. Keeping that from happening had directed his days and haunted his nights. Fear of losing her had hung over him like a sharpened blade. He'd been sure that no feeling could be worse.

He wasn't ready for this.

Staring down at this little creature, holding the squirming body in his hands, Viktor's whole being ached like an open wound. A wound he knew instinctively would never heal.

And for the first time in his life, he understood what it felt like to be truly afraid.

Chapter Six

"He's something, isn't he?"

Kat watched the little miracle suckling at her breast. "He sure is." She'd dreamed of her baby's birth for months, and for months she'd expected to go through the experience alone. The fact that Viktor was here with her now, that he had delivered their child into the world was more special to her than she could say.

On the drive to the hospital, she tried to tell him she wanted to be more, live for something more. At the time she'd said it, she didn't really understand exactly what she was after. The yearning had been vague, a hunger she didn't know quite how to satisfy or explain. But right now, looking at their child, she felt she'd found the answer. Her child was more. He was the future. And although she already sensed this new adventure would require more of her than she ever knew she had, she'd give everything for him and then some.

She glanced up at Viktor. A floor lamp shone from behind him, making his hair glow as if it was a halo of light. Although shadows the shade of bruises cupped under his eyes, his lips turned up at the corners in a hint of a smile.

No matter what they'd been through, no matter what the future brought, she was grateful he was here for this moment. It was something that could never be taken away, something they could share forever.

He glanced up from the baby and raised his brows. "Have you considered names?"

She looked back down at her son. In the months since she'd believed Viktor had died, she'd obsessed over choosing a name. But although she'd tried every name in the baby name book to see how it felt on her tongue, she'd really only seriously considered two. "Danny. I want to call him Danny."

"Daniel." He said the name DAN-ee-el, the way it was pronounced in Rasnovia.

"Of course."

"My father's name."

She nodded and watched his face for a sign of emotion. She wasn't sure how Viktor would take the idea of naming his son after the father he'd lost to an assassin so many years ago. She hadn't thought he'd ever know the name she'd picked out for their child. But now that she was finally holding their baby in her arms, she knew it was the right name. And she didn't know how she could ever pick another. "You like it?"

"I don't know."

She let out a breath she wasn't aware she'd been holding. There had been another choice. The choice she'd gone back and forth about. "I wanted to name him Viktor, but somehow…I just couldn't."

He nodded, as though he understood without her having to say more.

Of course, he probably did. Viktor had lost so many loved ones. He understood loss better than any person should have to. "I thought you'd like that he had your father's name. I thought you would think it honored him."

"I do."

"Then why aren't you sure?"

He paced across the floor. His shoulders weren't slumped, yet his posture wasn't as proud and vital as usual. He looked tired.

As tired as she felt. She looked down at the baby, suddenly aware that he'd stopped suckling. He slept against her breast, mouth open. Even he was exhausted. "Maybe we should just sleep on it tonight. If you don't like it, we can try to think of something else tomorrow."

"No, I like it. I just…"

She could guess the problem. The same reason she hadn't been able to bear to call her son Viktor. "You're afraid giving him the name will also give him the fate."

"It's ridiculous. I know."

"No, it's not."

He stopped in mid-stride and turned to face her. "I don't want him to have anything to do with what's going on in Rasnovia. If we give him my father's name, it's as if we're giving him a place in the monarchy. A role to be born into."

"He's your son. He's royalty whether you want him to be or not."

"I know. I just keep thinking that if I can get you away from here. Hide you. Change your identity, the two of you will be safe. You can have a good life."

Her stomach tensed in a very different kind of cramp. "The two of us?"

"You'll be safer somewhere away from me. At least until this is all over."

"'All over'? What does that mean?"

"Until Rasnovia is no longer in turmoil. Until there's no more threat."

"Your country has been in turmoil for…ever."

He shifted his gaze to the side.

Her throat ached. He didn't want to look at her, because he didn't want to acknowledge exactly what his plan meant. For her. For him. For them.

"So the whole marriage thing…you've changed your mind."

"You're the one who didn't want to get married."

He was right. Yet now that the offer was off the table, she wanted nothing more than to have it back. Even if they weren't truly partners, a sliver of what she hoped they could have together was better than nothing at all. Wasn't it?

She rubbed her eyes with the back of her hand. "So Danny and I…we would have a life of hiding?"

"You would have a *life*."

She understood the rest without him saying the words. *A life, as opposed to death.*

She trailed her fingertips over Danny's head, the wisps of his silken brown hair soft on her skin. She could already see the sheen of sandy hair under the dark brown he was born with. And even though conventional wisdom said all babies' eyes appeared to be blue when they were born, she knew he'd have his father's eyes, as well. "And while we're having a life, what are you planning to do?"

"I have a responsibility to Rasnovia. I can't let my people down."

"You're going to…what…start a civil war?" The thought inspired a quake deep in her bones.

"I hope not. Not if I can do things a different way."

"A different way?"

"The rebellion in Rasnovia is a small fringe group. They never could have executed something as complicated as the bombing in the palace. They never could have pulled off the coup. And yet they did."

"You said the soldiers were mercenaries. An army for hire."

"But where did the rebels get the money to hire them? They have never been well organized. They have never been well financed."

"So you think someone else is behind this? Someone is paying the bills and calling the shots?"

"Yes."

"Who?"

"If I knew that, I might have a chance to fight this."

"So that's what you're going to do? You're going to find out."

"Yes."

"How?"

"I need to get in touch with Flint, Jackson and Akeem."

"Have you tried calling Flint and Lora Leigh again?" Worry for her friends flared inside her like a fire getting a dose of oxygen.

"Yes. When you and the baby were asleep. They're okay."

"What happened? Why was the phone dead?"

"The line was cut. I finally reached Flint on his cell phone."

"The deputy and those other soldiers?"

He nodded. "When they realized we weren't there, they must have abandoned their original plans and started checking the hospitals. Either that, or they spotted us driving away."

Either way they'd succeeded in tracking her down.

"Flint and Lora Leigh were lucky they didn't cut the lines or jam their cell phones before Flint could ring his men. They might not be so lucky next time."

"Do you think the rebels have people watching the ranch?"

"I would. And Akeem's and Jackson's homes, too. That's why I'm not sure how I can arrange a meeting."

She thought back to what she'd been doing when those men had strode into the barn. Her life on the ranch seemed so far away now. Her day-to-day duties of grooming horses like distant memories. But even though her world had changed dramatically over the last twenty-four hours, the rest of the world was still marching on. "Tomorrow is Sunday. I know where to find Flint and Akeem. Maybe even Jackson."

"Where?"

"Akeem's auction house. There's a big sale tomorrow afternoon."

"Then I'll have to be there, as well."

"You're going to plan what to do next? You, Flint, Jackson and Akeem?"

"Yes." He looked at her out of the corner of his eye.

She knew what his answer would be before she asked, but she pushed ahead anyway. "Can I help?"

"You just had a baby, Kat. Your duty is to him."

"I'm not talking about shirking that duty. I just want to help. I want to do something."

"I know. You want to be a partner."

She gritted her teeth. How dare he throw her words back at her? Words whose meaning to her he obviously didn't understand? "He's my son, damn it. I want to do whatever I can to protect him, too."

A muscle along his jaw flexed. "This isn't the same as buying dinner, Kat."

"What do you think I am, a child? I'm not saying I'm going to march to war with you, carrying Danny in a baby sling. I just want to help you get to the bottom of this. When the fighting starts, I promise Danny and I will disappear. Besides, what were you planning to do? Leave us here in the motel with no way to defend ourselves?" She knew she was being manipulative, but she also knew Viktor well enough to know it would work. And besides, he'd asked for it.

He blew a breath between tight lips. "All right. Tomorrow we'll all go to the auction house. After we talk to the others, we'll hit the road. We'll find a place for you and Daniel to hide, agreed?"

She gave a reluctant nod.

"It's the only way I can make sure you'll be safe, Kat. You and Daniel. I've lost everything. I can't lose you."

"What you're talking about…you might never see us again."

He bobbed his head in a resigned nod. "But I'll know you're out there. That's all that matters." He stopped by the bed and smoothed his hand over her hair. "So it's settled?"

Maybe it was. And maybe disappearing was the only thing she and the baby could do. But that didn't stop the doubt from niggling at the back of Kat's mind. "I hid last time, and they found me. What makes you think this time will be different?"

"We'll erase all ties between us. The rebels will have nothing to follow."

"Erase all ties." The words made her want to cry. So that's what all this had come down to. Viktor had come back to life just so he could erase all ties between them. For a moment, she'd really felt like she had a family, Viktor, Danny and her. Something special. Something to live up to. And although she knew deep down that she and Viktor couldn't have some sort of happy ever after in their future, hearing him talk about erasing all ties brought that reality home. And facing that reality once again threatened to rip her heart in two.

She pushed down the mash of feelings welling inside and met his eyes. Protecting Danny. That's all that mattered. In that, she and Viktor were united.

And that would have to be enough.

AKEEM ABDUL'S TEXAS Double A Auctions sprawled on the outskirts of Houston like a palace built to pay homage to the cult of horse trading. The main building was shaped like a small American football stadium, and housed the main auction ring as well as exercising arenas designed for bidders to get an up close look at animals they might want to buy. The building was also home to a dozen or more vendors, selling everything from saddles to feed supplements to T-shirts for horse-crazy girls. And in the far back corner hid the office complex where Akeem managed his businesses.

The other two buildings were filled with stalls, wash racks, grooming areas and two more exercise areas. Every facility a horse buyer or seller could need. It was the biggest auction house in Texas and quickly becoming the premiere equine auction house in the nation, even overtaking some of the thoroughbred sales venues in the east. Akeem had worked hard to build his auction business, and like the other members of The Aggie Four, he'd faced his share of opposition, from good old boys who took exception to the success of the "Texas Sheik."

Having had to rely on a taxi to get them to the auction house, the first thing Viktor and Kat did was locate Flint's trailers in the parking lot behind barn two. Alongside a plethora of other dual-wheeled pickups and trailers, Flint's rigs took up several spaces, even though according to Kat, he hadn't taken as many horses to the sale as usual. Kat located the hidden key and let them into the six-horse trailer in which he'd found her hiding from the mercenaries two days before.

Viktor checked his watch. Flint had given them the location of his stalls over the phone and had assured them Akeem and Jackson would be at the sale, as well. Now there was nothing to do but get ready and wait. Arriving to the meeting early would only expose them to more danger of being spotted. He glanced at Kat.

"It's almost time to go, isn't it?" Kat sat on the edge of the trailer's gooseneck, caramel eyes still tired after the spotty rest she'd gotten last night.

She cradled the little bundle to her breast, his mouth attached and suckling.

For a moment, Viktor just watched her, unable to find the words. She'd always had a sexy body, full curves, a sensual way of moving, a soft scent he couldn't breathe in deeply enough. But now? Her breasts were fuller than he could imagine, her body so lush, it was all he could do to keep himself from touching her. And the idea that the body that he'd always found so sexy was also nourishing his son made him want to gape in awe. "Uh, no. We're fine for time. We'll leave when he's done."

"How can we be sure the deputy isn't here? Or a soldier? You said yourself they're probably watching Flint, Akeem and Jackson."

He'd considered that probability, and he didn't intend to leave anything to chance.

"Do you think you and Daniel would fit in one of those two-wheeled carts?" He nodded at the green monstrosity leaning up against a wall in the tiny space.

Kat's eyebrows arched. "You're going to wheel us in like a load of manure?"

"I was thinking more along the lines of a load of hay, but yes."

She considered for a moment. "We'd fit. I think I'd like to have him in his seat, though. You know,

with something between him and the cart." She
pursed her lips together. "How about you?"

"Me?"

"You don't look the part of a hand."

Too bad he'd left the hat he'd used at the
hospital in the men's room. "I was hoping I could
come up with something of Flint's."

She twisted on her perch and pointed behind her.
"There's a whole extra wardrobe back in the gooseneck there."

As Kat finished nursing the baby, Viktor went
to work. Within a few minutes, Viktor had
jammed a Stetson on his head, silver belly and
new from the box. A denim shirt replaced his
button-down, and a pair of Wranglers hugged his
thighs a little too snuggly.

The baby now secured in the bucket car seat
they'd bought on the way, Kat looked him up and
down. "Nice. Rugged, independent, tight jeans.
People make a big deal over princes, but cowboys
really have it going on."

He didn't know how she still had her sense of
humor after all she'd been through, but he was
glad she did. "Get in the manure cart."

She shot him a smart-ass smile and crawled
gingerly into the cart, curling on her side around
the baby. She raised the seat's visor over his head.
"Okay, we're ready."

Viktor covered them with a horse blanket. Now or never. He grasped the cart's handle and pushed it out from the space between the parked trailers and toward the barn. With two, nearly bike-sized wheels, the cart pushed easily.

The barn bustled with activity. Grooms leading horses clopping from the wash rack, their conditioner-scented tails leaving a trail of drips on the concrete aisle. Girls on stools sectioning off unruly manes with rubber bands to show off a horse's top line to best advantage. Trainers lunging horses for prospective buyers.

Viktor assumed a cowboy's rocking gate and tried to blend with his surroundings. The scent of wood shavings warmed the air, a hint of ammonia and manure sprinkled in the mix like seasoning. It was a good smell, a clean smell. It reminded Viktor of windblown valleys and hard work.

In Rasnovia the horse scene was powered by warmbloods, big sturdy horse breeds that excelled in dressage and jumping. Here in Texas, the quarter horse ruled, competing in horse shows and rodeo, cutting cattle and working on the ranch. The quarter horse was the ultimate tool of the cowboy. And thanks to breeding programs like that at the Diamondback Ranch the thoroughbred industry was thriving in Texas, as well. But in the end, it was all the same. Good people and good horses. It reminded him of all Rasnovia and the U.S. shared.

And how vital it was that he make sure his country and its dream of democracy survived.

He spotted Flint from across one of the workout pens. The cowboy was wearing a straw hat, much like the one Viktor had left in the hospital restroom. A silver-encrusted bridle thrown over one shoulder, he gestured with his hands in an animated conversation with another horseman.

A horseman who seemed very familiar.

A gray Stetson blended with the thick gray hair underneath. A striped shirt covered broad shoulders and was tucked into the usual pair of Wranglers. A belt buckle half the size of Texas adorned his waist. He turned to the side, a scowl marring his sharp-featured face.

Lawrence McElroy.

Viktor ducked his head so his hat's brim shielded his face. He didn't think the man saw him. He hoped not. "Hold on, Kat. We have a change of plans."

Heart knocking against his ribs, he maneuvered the cart around the opposite side of the round pen and down a side aisle. Dodging a girl carrying a box of Corgi pups, he negotiated a maze of side aisles before reaching a row of empty stalls along the barn's far end.

He stood still for a moment, waiting for the

thud of boots, the jingle of spurs hitting concrete. Nothing but the normal sounds of country music on a tinny radio and the hum of horses and human voices met his ears.

The horse blanket stirred. "Viktor?" The corner pulled back and a questioning eye the color of caramel peered up at him.

"We've got problems at Flint's stalls."

"The deputy?"

He gave his head a shake. "An old friend of ours, only he's not much of a friend. His name is McElroy."

"The owner of Stone Creek?"

"You know him?"

"I've seen him around."

A prickle assaulted the back of Flint's neck. Kat had only been at the Diamondback ranch for about five months. He hadn't been aware McElroy had made a problem of himself that recently. "What do you know about him?"

"Just that he blames Flint for buying Diamond Daddy out from under him. He's been trying to get Flint back ever since."

Viktor nodded. Unfortunately it was nothing he didn't already know.

Kat shifted in the cart. Lifting her head, she tried to peek out at their surroundings. "You think he might be part of the rebellion in Rasnovia?"

"He has the money and he's done a few things in the past that have shown he likes to mess with The Aggie Four." He clamped his jaw and shook his head. "Probably not, though. Most of what he's done is mess up horse deals. Not quite the same as financing the overthrow of a country."

"Maybe he's not working alone."

"That's more possible. The thing I'm most worried about is him recognizing me. I have to figure out a way to contact Flint and the others. There's no way we can meet in Flint's stall aisle. Not with McElroy around."

"How about Akeem's offices?"

He pictured the office complex where Akeem ran his business. Attached to the auction house itself, it had been a bustle of staff, bidders and sellers on the last auction day he'd attended. "Too busy."

"I've got it. The lounge."

His mind drew a blank. "Lounge?"

"Akeem had it built this spring. It's a luxury lounge in the main building overlooking the auction ring. You should see it. It's set aside for high-dollar bidders who don't like to mix with the rabble in the stands. And it has a well-stocked bar, which Akeem says is helpful in loosening big pocketbooks."

Funny. Akeem had always joked about making that type of addition to the auction house to bring in more high rollers. He'd finally done it. The horse auction equivalent of the club level at Reliant Stadium.

He glanced down at his watch. "Bidding starts at two. That's in fifteen minutes. Won't someone be using the lounge?"

"Not for the afternoon auction. Only youth activity horses are on this afternoon's slate. Akeem doesn't open the lounge for family auctions."

Viktor smiled. Leave it to Akeem to be judicious in what pocketbooks he chose to lubricate. His friend had always had a soft spot for kids. "Then the lounge it is."

He pushed the cart down a long aisle and made a left into the wide walkway that connected the barns with the auction house. He dodged people, dogs and the occasional horse, and finally came upon the auction ring itself.

A little bigger than the standard round pen, the ring was surrounded by a mini grandstand. Where many horse auction venues forced bidders to sit on simple bleachers, Akeem provided seats like those found in a major league baseball park. Half the seats were already full and a steady stream of parents, children and their trainers shuffled into the rest. On the opposite side of the auction ring, vendors hawked their horsey wares next to the entrance to the office complex. Above, a bank of windows peered over the action.

"Excuse me, son. Where are you headed?" a gruff voice called out.

Viktor walked faster. McElroy's voice? He didn't think so. But the last thing he wanted was for someone to get a close look at him. The general public probably wouldn't recognize him, but certain horse people might.

"Son? Are you lost?" The sound of boots on concrete followed him. "Hey. We're getting ready for an auction here. Horses are on their way in. I can't have that cart stopping up my aisles."

Viktor stopped. Half turning his head, he got a glimpse of a heavyset man wearing a shirt that bore Texas Double A Auctions' logo. Someone who worked here. Viktor hoped he was a new hire. Keeping his face averted, Viktor summoned his best Texas drawl. "Mr. Abdul said he needed these blankets, so I brung 'em. Ask him what he wants to do with 'em."

"Take them back to the barn."

"He asked…sir."

The man shook his head and stalked to the cart. He squinted down at the insignia on the blanket. "Wait a second. This don't belong to Double A. Whose are these?" He reached for the blanket's corner.

Chapter Seven

Viktor lunged at the man's hand. Grabbing his wrist, he stopped his reach for the blanket. "Hands off, buddy."

The man looked up at him, shock written on his beefy face. "What the—"

"These belong to Diamondback Ranch. Mr. McKade wanted me to bring 'em to Mr. Abdul." He released the man's hand. "Don't grab what's not yours."

The man held his hand aloft and rubbed his wrist. He looked the blankets over, then narrowed his eyes at Viktor.

Viktor tilted his chin down, angling his hat to shield at least part of his face. The man was looking a little too closely. He had to get rid of him. "I want to talk to Mr. Abdul. I don't have time to be playing games. Mr. McKade is waiting on me."

"Then go on. I'll take them to Akeem."

"So you can say I didn't do my job? No way. I ain't moving until I talk to Mr. Abdul."

For a moment, Viktor wasn't sure if the guy was going to fetch Akeem or just try out his bucket-sized fists on Viktor's face. Even though Viktor knew how to defend himself, the guy had a good thirty-five pounds on him. The result wouldn't be pretty.

The man gave him a good snarl. "Oh, hell." He spun on his boot heel and set off across the ring.

Viktor's legs felt rubbery with relief. So far, so good. As long as Akeem was suspicious enough about the situation that he checked it out himself, they would be okay. If he just told the guy to deal with it, they were in deep trouble.

"Viktor?" The whisper rose from under the blanket.

"We're okay. He's going to get Akeem." At least he hoped that's what would happen. He watched the heavyset man reach the office complex and disappear inside. Thirty seconds later, Akeem Abdul poked his head into the auction house and peered across the ring. A smile curved over the sheik's lips and he motioned to Viktor.

"Akeem's here. We're all set." Viktor circled behind the stands and joined his friend.

Akeem held out a hand. "I'm grateful you could bring those blankets to me."

"I heard you might want them in the lounge?"

"Excellent idea." Akeem led the way to a back staircase hidden from the rest of the auction hoopla. There, Viktor peeled back the horse blanket and Kat climbed out of the cart.

Akeem took Kat into his arms in a brief hug, then peered under the visor. His dark eyes gleamed. "He's really something. Viktor, Kat, I'm so happy for you. Now we'd better get him upstairs. This place is crazy this close to auction. Someone could wander back here any minute."

Viktor nodded. The sooner they had at least a locked door between them and whoever might be out there looking for them, the better he'd feel. "Lead the way."

He grasped the baby carrier and toted his son up the stairs behind Akeem and Kat. Akeem unlocked a door on the second level and gestured them inside. He bolted the door behind them.

Viktor took a look around the room. The bank of windows he'd noticed from below provided a crystal clear view of not only the ring where the bidding took place, but the entire auction house. "One-way glass?"

Akeem nodded. "Nothing but the best for my bidders."

Nothing but the best indeed. A bar flanked one wall, stocked with single malt scotch, fine wine and some good down-home bourbon for those who were cowboy through and through. Cocktail tables and leather chairs lined the area near the windows, each complete with a small keyboard for recording bids, like something found in an auction house for fine art and precious gems. Even the walls were luxuriously appointed, gilded frames setting off remarkable paintings of famous horses. He spotted Flint's Triple Crown winning stud horse, Diamond Daddy, standing proudly above the bar. Viktor had been in a lot of auction houses over the years, but he'd never seen anything quite this posh. At least not for horses.

"Something to drink?" Akeem offered.

Kat asked for water. Viktor shook his head. "Can you ring up Flint and Jackson? Tell them to meet here?"

"Certainly."

As Akeem stepped into an office to make the calls, Viktor stepped to the window and looked down on the auction ring. The stands were almost filled now. Sharply dressed families. Grooms who looked like they didn't have enough change to buy a new pair of jeans, let alone a horse. Some trainers he recognized. No deputies or mercenaries that he could pick out. But no Flint and Jackson, either.

Suddenly he needed to pace. Instead he faced Akeem. "Does Jackson know I'm here?"

"Yes."

"Is he—"

"Angry? Yes. With you and with me. But he'll get over it. Ysabel will see to it."

"Ysabel. Kat said Jackson finally came to his senses and married her."

Akeem nodded. "And they have a little one of their own on the way."

"No kidding." Viktor clapped Akeem on the back. "I hear you've given away a diamond ring of your own recently. One of your grandfather's collection?"

Akeem nodded. A smile spread across his lips. "And Taylor has finally agreed to set a date."

"When?"

"Next summer. She wants to wait until she graduates and can get a foothold in the world of accounting. Now if we can tie this mess up before then, I would be a happy man."

The doorknob rattled.

A dose of adrenaline slammed into Viktor's bloodstream. Akeem straightened, his smile gone. His hand moved, and for the first time, Viktor noticed he was armed. He looked at Viktor and nodded past the bar.

Viktor grabbed the handle of the baby seat, and he and Kat slipped to the other side of the bar where a door led to a small conference room. They ducked inside, leaving the door open a crack to listen.

Out in the lounge, they could hear Akeem open the door. The low hum of voices reached them, Akeem's and another with a higher pitch. Maybe two. A second later, the door thunked closed again. "All clear."

Viktor stepped back into the room, keeping Kat and the baby behind him, just in case.

Flint's sister, Taylor, stood by Akeem's side. A little boy hovered behind her, his arm looped around her leg. She kissed Akeem, then smiled at Viktor. "Viktor. I can't tell you how grateful I am that you're alive."

Viktor crossed the room and gave Taylor a hug. "Taylor, I can't tell you how grateful I am that Akeem finally proposed. I'm no romantic, but I knew back in our college days that the two of you belonged together."

"You're the biggest romantic I know, Prince." Taylor gave him a teasing look. "And you should have told us."

"I think I did."

"Well, then we should have listened," Akeem added.

Taylor looked past Viktor. "Kat. I always wondered how you fit into all of this. At first, I even thought you and Akeem…" She focused on the baby seat. Her eyes widened. "You had the baby."

Kat grinned. "Do you want to hold him?"

"Do I?" She raced to Kat's side, her little boy in tow. "Look, Christopher. You have a little guy to play with."

"Can I wrestle with him?"

Taylor laughed. Kat joined in. "I think you'll have to wait until he's a little bigger."

"Okay."

A soft knock sounded on the door. Viktor, Kat and the baby went through their hiding routine once again. When they emerged from the conference room, Jackson Champion met Viktor's gaze. His lips flattened to a hard line.

Viktor held up a hand. "I know. I'm sorry."

"I figure you had your reasons. Like some fool notion you were protecting us."

Viktor nodded and offered his hand. Jackson pulled him close and clapped his other hand on Viktor's back. "If you ever do that again, I'll string you up."

Jackson and Ysabel joined Taylor in mooning over the baby. Ysabel certainly carried a glow about her, and Viktor could detect a definite baby bulge.

After going through the whole knock-on-the-door routine again, Flint and Lora Leigh finally joined the party.

A few minutes later, the lion's part of the mooning was over, and the baby was sucking at his mother's breast. The chant of the auctioneer bled through the windows as a slow parade of horseflesh moved through the ring below.

Viktor looked at the men who made up The Aggie Four and their women. Each of them had paid a price. Each of them still faced a risk. And each of them was here, eager to help.

If any men and women could make a difference in this mess, it would be them.

Viktor gave them the story of all that had happened to him in Rasnovia, a shortened version of what he'd explained to Kat. It was easier this time. As if already having told it had worn off the raw edges. As if feeling Kat's gaze on him, steady and supportive, gave him what he needed to live through the memory again.

When he finished, his friends were silent. Flint broke the stillness. "I can't say what I would have chosen to do in your shoes, Viktor. But I'm glad you're here with us now."

Jackson nodded. "These last few months have been tough. But if we stick together—" he shot Akeem a glance "—all *four* of us, we can straighten this damn mess out."

Viktor exchanged looks with the three men. "Kat filled me in on what has been happening with all of you, and I'm convinced it all leads back to the coup in Rasnovia."

Jackson nodded. "An agent by the name of Keller

told me the FBI traced one of the men involved in smuggling the dirty bomb back to Rasnovia."

Even though Viktor had been halfway around the world when the dirty bomb had been smuggled into the United States aboard one of Jackson's ships, he'd seen the story on CNN. In the past day, Kat had filled him in on all Jackson and Ysabel had endured as a result.

"So that proves it," Kat said. "And there was corruption in law enforcement related to the bomb, too, wasn't there?"

"In one case. You suspect more?"

Kat filled them all in on their experiences with Deputy Bobby Lee Stubfield.

"I've been thinking about good ol' Bobby Lee," said Flint. "It seems mighty suspicious that he was the only deputy to respond to a shooting. There might be others in the system that are on the take."

"Others?"

"Other deputies. Maybe a dispatcher. Hard to say."

"It is also someone with more money than God."

Viktor shot Ysabel a questioning look. "Why do you say that?"

"It is what the detective told me when he thought I was about to die. More money than God," she repeated.

Kat cleared her throat. "Like whoever could afford to finance a coup d'état."

"And there's more," Ysabel continued. She dipped a hand into her bag and pulled out a small notebook. The giant marquis diamond engagement ring and matching wedding band glittered on her finger. "There is a personal component to all the attacks."

"A personal component?" Lora Leigh echoed in a question, but she was already nodding her head.

"*Si,* I've been keeping track of all the people involved in the attacks on members of The Aggie Four. Whoever is behind this seems to know too much about each of you for there to be any other explanation. See?" She displayed a page full of names and relationships and events. Everything from Flint's problems at his ranch to Taylor's son's kidnapping to the dirty bomb involving Jackson's shipping company.

Viktor leaned forward with the rest of The Aggie Four and studied the lists. Leave it to Ysabel. Viktor doubted Jackson could run his shipping empire without her, on a professional level, or his life, on a personal one. "So you think everything's related. The personal attacks, the money to pay off law enforcement and others, and the takeover of my country."

"I do."

Viktor nodded. "So do we."

Kat shifted the baby to her shoulder and started patting his back. "If it's someone who knows the four of you both personally and professionally and has a lot of money, that narrows things down, right?"

"Not enough," Flint said.

Viktor agreed. "The four of us have been running in many of the same social and business circles since college at Texas A&M. We know a lot of the same people." And if there was a single thing Viktor had learned in the years he'd spent attending schools in the U.S. and Europe and traveling all over the globe in preparation for the throne of Rasnovia, it was that the world was a very small place.

Akeem tented his fingers, tapping them on his lips. "The questions are who and why."

"And what to do about it," added Jackson.

Viktor had been mulling those questions nearly nonstop since his talk with Kat. And after arriving at the auction house, he wondered if he needed to add another name to his list. He eyed Flint. "What did Lawrence McElroy want?"

"Just being his usual pain-in-the-ass self. Why? You think he might have expanded his hobby of meddling in the horse business to include meddling in the political structure of foreign countries?"

"I don't know. I just have a bad feeling about him. It doesn't make sense, does it?"

"It might make more sense than you think." Jackson motioned to the glass and the auction outside. "Our friend McElroy has recently bought up a large number of shares of Champion Shipping after the stock price dropped. And I was talking to Deke Norton the other day, and it seems McElroy's done the same with Norton International."

"Interesting," Akeem said, nodding thoughtfully. He glanced at Viktor. "Who else do you have a bad feeling about?"

"Amal Jabar." Viktor had met the Saudi Sheik and horse trader through Akeem, and he watched carefully for his friend's reaction.

Akeem's expression didn't change. "If this was a month ago, I would tell you you're crazy. But now..."

"Why?" Viktor felt his pulse quicken. "What has happened with Jabar?"

"He's been selling assets."

"Horses?"

"Horses, land, stock. Everything. And yet he tells me all is well. I have to wonder what he's hiding."

"So Jabar is selling and McElroy is buying. What does that mean?" Kat asked.

"Too bad Deke has no cause to be buying youth

horses." Jackson nodded at the auction on the other side of the glass. "If anyone might have an idea about what all of this means, it's him."

Viktor needed to make sure Kat and Daniel were safe, first and foremost. But if there was a way to see Deke… He shook his head. The Aggie Four's old mentor didn't know he was alive, and it was better that he stay in the dark. Viktor was already putting enough of the people he cared about at risk. He didn't want to expand that list even more.

"So we have some ideas about who, what about the why and what to do about it?" Jackson said.

Viktor cleared his throat. "I don't have any more answers than that. But I do have a plan."

Flint slapped his hands on his denim-clad thighs. "Spill it."

"First, I need someone to go to Rasnovia. Someone with connections inside the country. We need to know what's going on over there. My interior minister, Toma Stanislav, is running the show." Viktor paused. He still couldn't believe Toma had betrayed him so utterly. And worse, that he hadn't seen it coming.

He cleared his throat and continued. "But it might be helpful to know what special interests are wielding power behind the scenes." He glanced at Akeem. When it had come to smuggling Kat out of the country, he'd chosen Akeem over the other two members of The Aggie Four precisely because he had the most connections in Rasnovia. Being a sheik instead of a high-profile American didn't hurt in this political climate, either. And more than the others, he was the best candidate to get the information they needed now.

Akeem dropped his hands to his sides and nodded.

"It might be dangerous," Viktor warned.

Akeem looked to Taylor. "Christopher…"

Taylor looked less than thrilled, but she nodded. "There isn't a chance Christopher is going anywhere near that country. Not until all this is over. And of course, you know I'm not leaving him for a second. Besides, you'll be able to find out more if you go alone."

Kat had told him about Taylor's son's kidnapping. Now that he was a parent, he could fully understand the horror she'd gone through. As well as Taylor's refusal to let the boy out of her sight. If someone took Daniel…

Akeem turned his dark eyes back to Viktor. "I'll book a flight out tomorrow."

"How about the political implications, as far as the United States is concerned?" Jackson asked. "It would be interesting to know exactly who is behind lobbying efforts to convince Uncle Sam to recognize the new government."

"Are you volunteering?" Viktor asked.

"Damn straight."

"I'll clear your schedule and book the flight to D.C." Ysabel said, the tone of her voice efficient as usual. "Two seats. I'm going with you."

"What about us?" Lora Leigh asked.

"I need you to do some poking around inside the county sheriff's department. Houston PD, too, if you can. It sure would be helpful to know who we can trust in law enforcement and who we can't."

"Not a problem," Flint said. "I think it's safe to put Bobby Lee Stubfield on the can't. If we can nail down any more names for that list, we'll let you know."

Lora Leigh rose to stand next to her husband. "If you need a place, somewhere you can disappear, we have land in Florida, fruit orchards, a bird sanctuary and the like. Might be a nice place for a baby. Some of the property is not tied to the ranch."

Viktor focused on Lora Leigh, trying not to notice the frown on Kat's face. "I'll need directions. And a car. Something that can't be traced to any of us. At least not easily."

"I have cousins in the area who are trying to sell a car."

Jackson grinned at his bride. "Honey, you have dozens of cousins who are trying to sell dozens of cars."

She shrugged at his teasing. "Actually, I do. I'll arrange for someone to drop a car off for you. Here?"

"That would be perfect. Thank you. I will give you cash."

Jackson held up a hand. "Keep it. If you're officially dead, you'll need it."

Jackson was right. He had already burned through a stack of cash at the motel. Once he was dry, he couldn't draw on his accounts in Rasnovia, accounts probably already liquidated by Toma and his people. "Thank you. There's one more thing. My gun. I had to leave it in the pickup, Flint. I didn't want to go back, not after Stubfield and the mercenaries were sniffing around. I hope that doesn't come back to bite you." A weapon that had shot two men found hidden in a truck registered to him might cause a serious problem for Flint, even with honest law enforcement.

"I reported the truck stolen. I hope that's enough to convince them I had nothing to do with the shootings, if they do find it. If not, I have a very good lawyer."

"It won't go that far," Viktor assured, for Lora Leigh's sake as much as Flint's. If it did, Viktor would come back to life and tell the whole story. His friends were facing enough danger, enough risk. Exactly the reason he had decided not to ask them to replace the pistol he'd left in the truck. He'd bought one illegally before, he could do it again.

"Kat? Viktor?" said Taylor. "I don't know that I can do too much to help, but if something goes wrong, remember I'm here. I already have one little guy. I sure wouldn't mind having a baby in my arms again."

"Thank you." Viktor looked at the three other members of The Aggie Four and their women. People he could rely on. People he could trust. And he had a feeling before this was over, his bond with each would be tested more than any of them could imagine.

TWO HOURS after they'd finished their talk and Jackson, Ysabel, Flint and Lora Leigh had made their exit from the lounge. Viktor and Kat said their goodbyes to Akeem, Taylor and her son Christopher and took the stairs back down to the auction house's main level. Ysabel had assured them a car would be waiting for them in the parking lot in less than two hours, and Kat was sure she would deliver. Ysabel's power to get things done was truly amazing. Jackson's, too, if the wedding he'd organized single-handedly for his bride was any indication.

The cart waited at the bottom of the staircase. The thought of climbing under those stifling horse blankets again made Kat's nose tickle and skin itch. But the alternative of being spotted was worse. She set Danny's seat in the cart and was about to climb in beside him when Viktor grabbed her arm.

He held up a silent finger.

She could hear it, too. Male voices coming their way.

Viktor grabbed the baby from the cart. Moving back under the steps, he motioned for her to follow. They slipped between a vending machine and the slope of the staircase above.

The steady strike of cowboy boots grew louder, each step accompanied by the ching of a spur rowel hitting concrete. Cigarette smoke tinted the air. "Francine's has the best in Houston," a male voice boomed.

"How far?" The second voice carried an accent. Middle Eastern, probably. It reminded Kat of the slight tint Akeem still had, despite all the years he'd spent in the United States.

"Close."

"And it is quiet? We can talk business?"

"Sure can."

The men's footsteps moved away. The singsong of the auctioneer drowned out the men's plans. Kat shifted her shoes uneasily. "That was close."

Viktor said nothing.

She twisted in the tight space to get a look at his face.

Frown lines dug into his forehead. A muscle worked under the stubble on his chin.

Something had him worried. Something more than two men deciding where to eat. "What is it?"

"That was Amal Jabar. And more importantly, Warren Gregory."

She recognized the first name from the conversation they'd just had with the rest of The Aggie Four. But the second name meant nothing to her. "Who is Warren Gregory?"

"He's a representative of a very large, very powerful corporation. At least he used to be."

"A representative? Like a salesman?"

"A little. Gregory visited me and my mother in Rasnovia a few years ago. He made us an offer."

"An offer? What kind of offer?"

He let out a derisive laugh. "As it turns out, an offer we couldn't refuse."

Chapter Eight

"What do you mean, an offer you couldn't refuse? This doesn't have something to do with bloody sheets and the severed head of a prized stallion, does it?" Kat whispered.

If the topic wasn't so serious, Viktor would chuckle. "No, it's not the scene from *The Godfather*. Gregory wanted us to mortgage Rasnovia's future in exchange for bridges, dams, power plants and most of all, an oil pipeline."

"But you've made improvements like that with The Aggie Four Foundation, with the exception of the pipeline."

"Exactly. And as a result, Rasnovia's infrastructure is owned by the people and operated for the good of the people. And the country isn't in debt to a foreign corporation who demands even more contracts and resources flow their way, whether their work benefits the people or not, which a pipeline wouldn't." Just the thought of Gregory's pipeline proposal still made him angry. Rasnovia did not need a pipeline plowing through the middle of the country, eating up prime agricultural land in a nation that needed every bit of that it could get. The whole project had been for the benefit of multinational energy companies.

"And if a country this guy approaches says no? Like you did?"

"An assassination. A coup d'état. A revolution. A war. Whatever is needed to force a government to comply or to change to one who will."

"You think this Warren Gregory might be backing the rebels who took over the government?"

"I think it's likely."

"But why would a man like that be here at a horse auction?"

"Good question. He's not a horseman. But Jabar deals with horses. Maybe Gregory came to the auction to meet with him. A better question might be why is he talking business with Jabar?"

"Akeem said Jabar was selling assets."

Viktor nodded. "I'm guessing Gregory is trying to convince him to put his new liquidity into the construction business in Rasnovia."

"You're guessing? It seems like an open-and-shut case to me."

Viktor only wished the scorecard were that simple and clear. And that he didn't have any kind of emotional stake clouding his view of it. "Jabar knows some questionable people, it's true. But all four of us have done business with him over the years. Akeem knows him pretty well. I guess I don't want to believe he's involved in this."

"Maybe he's not. Maybe Gregory is just trying to get him involved."

"I would pay a lot to know."

"So let's go to the restaurant and ask Gregory what he's up to."

Viktor shot her a fleeting grin. "You're kidding, right?"

"No."

"If he is behind the coup, and he knows I'm alive, things could get bad fast. There might not be a place either one of us can hide."

"What if we could do it without him seeing you?"

He had a bad feeling he knew what she was suggesting. And he didn't want her involved in this. He wanted her and Daniel far away and safe. "Absolutely not."

"You haven't heard my idea."

"I can guess. You're going to talk to him for me."

She tilted her head as if considering the idea. "That's not what I had in mind, but if you think it will work—"

"No."

She shot him a little smile that he felt deep in

his gut. "I will get him alone, and *you* can have a word with him."

"Get him alone, how?"

"Have you been to Francine's?"

"No."

"Well, I have. It has two levels. The upper level is the restaurant itself, and the lower one is used for weddings and banquets and that sort of thing. On a Sunday, I'm betting it won't be in use. If the restroom on the main level is closed just when he needs to use it…"

"He'll have to go downstairs. Alone." Then it would be up to him to get answers from Gregory without letting the man know who he was. And on the off chance that it was Jabar who wandered down the steps, he could ask him, although the sheik was stronger, schooled in martial arts and harder to control. No, better stick to Gregory.

Viktor let out a sigh. He had to admit, the plan might work. If not for one thing. "I don't want you involved."

"Come on, Viktor. We can do this right now. Maybe we can get some answers."

"It's too dangerous. He could spot you."

"You can't do it by yourself. Who do you expect to help? Akeem? Flint? He won't recognize me. I can guarantee it."

She was right. Anyone else, Gregory would know. "What about Daniel?"

"You heard Taylor's offer. She's still upstairs. She can take care of Danny."

"This could get complicated. You just had a baby."

"How about you? You were caught in an explosion just months ago. You almost died."

Leave it to Kat to turn it around on him. "I'm fine." Except for scarring and some lingering pains, he had healed. Time did that. Rest did that. She hadn't even given herself a chance.

"And I am, too."

He looked at her out of the corner of his eye. Her skin was off color, shadows hung under her eyes, and yet there was still that fire about her, that determination, what he liked to call her American bravado. It got him every time. It made him want to straighten his spine, raise his chin and forge ahead, despite the odds against him.

He couldn't lose her.

"Listen, Viktor. I know you're worried about me." Her voice was soft, sincere.

Another side to her he loved. A side he wanted to hold close at night. A side he missed like a physical ache. "You don't know the half of it."

She brushed his comment aside with a wave of her hand. "I admit I'd like to curl up with Danny and sleep for a week. And I will, eventually, I promise. But it's going to be easier to make that happen, to keep our little guy safe if we know what's going on."

He opened his mouth to protest.

She pressed a finger to his lips and looked directly into his eyes, a melding of grit and softness. "Keeping Danny safe is up to both of us. Don't cut me out of that. We need to work together."

He pressed his lips into a hard line and tightened his grip on the baby carrier. Working together. That's what she had wanted all along. And maybe if he gave in, just this one time, that argument would be over.

He just hoped he didn't regret this.

GETTING KAT INVOLVED IN THIS was a horrid idea. But it was too late to change things now.

They had entered the restaurant separately, Kat slipping in the back employee entrance in search of an apron and a toilet plunger and Viktor strolling through the front door. He almost called her back, told her to forget the whole thing.

He wished he had.

He stepped into the entry. The place was as posh inside as the exterior had promised. White linen swathed tables set with silver and china. Soft strains of Beethoven rose over the clink of crystal wineglasses. The scent of what the sign outside called The Finest Beef In The Country teased the air. He nodded to the maître d' and slipped into the bar. Sitting in one of the plush chairs that served as barstools, he ordered a single malt and leaned back as if people watching, fitting in perfectly with the other patrons, thanks to one of the changes of clothing Jackson and Ysabel had left for them in the back of the late model Volvo.

It took him a moment to spot Gregory and Jabar on the far side of the dining room. Even though Viktor hadn't gotten a good look at the man in years, he'd recognized Warren Gregory's slender athletic frame, balding head and lack of chin immediately at the auction house. Watching him now, Viktor couldn't help but note the air of arrogance that hung around Gregory, as thick and oppressive as smog on a hot day.

Viktor took a sip from his glass. Raising the cut crystal into the air, he flagged down the bartender. "I'd like to send a bottle of this to the Gregory table."

The bartender's black eyes sharpened, probably imagining the tip that would accompany such a purchase. "A *bottle?*"

"Yes." He drew out his wallet and laid out a few crisp hundreds. "And I'd like to stay anonymous."

"Of course, sir."

Gregory didn't stand a chance with an entire bottle of single malt at his fingertips. Not only would he be forced to eventually take that bathroom break, but he'd be good and drunk when he did.

That could only help.

Viktor took another sip from his tumbler, savoring the flavor, hot and smooth. He hated to leave a half-full glass, but his part here was done. Now that the bottle was on its way, there was no point in risking the possibility of someone recognizing him.

Besides, he needed all his faculties intact if he was going to pull this off.

Leaving his glass and a good tip on the bar, he stood and wound his way through the quiet mumble of conversation and music until he located the stairs to the lower level. Back in the dining room, delighted exclamations rose from Gregory and Jabar. So far, so good. Now all there was to do was make his way to the downstairs restroom, and wait for Kat to herd the man his way.

He prayed this would work.

The lower level was quiet, the party rooms dark. A panel of windows stretched along the open space near the restrooms. A gazebo surrounded by gardens shimmered in the soft exterior lighting. The remnants of a wedding from the night before scattered the surface of a large tray on a rack at the edge of the room. A stray pillar from a cake.

A wilted boutonniere. A jumble of tulle-wrapped favors no one bothered to take home.

Viktor stepped to the tray and picked up the boutonniere. Two long pins protruded from the wrapped stem. He pulled them free and dropped them into the pocket of his jacket. Not much as far as weapons went, but he would have to make do. As long as he had the element of surprise on his side and Gregory wasn't armed, he should be okay.

Viktor ducked inside the restroom to begin his wait.

While the ballroom hadn't been totally cleaned after the weekend's festivities, lucky for Viktor, the restroom had. The sharp scent of lemon disinfectant greeted him. Lights gleamed on a clean marble vanity and brushed nickle faucets.

Two urinals were located on the opposite wall. The white fixtures floated in the center of a stretch of marble tile. No mirrors. No way for the user to see anyone approaching from behind.

Perfect.

He slipped into a bathroom stall built like a small room. The solid oak door reached all the way to the floor. Viktor stood just inside the door and began his wait.

He wasn't sure how much time had passed. Ten minutes? Thirty? When he could feel the air pressure change caused by the outside door swinging open.

Leather-soled boots sounded on marble.

Viktor tensed. Reaching into his jacket pocket, he took out the stick pins and aligned the sharp tips. He rested his fingers on the cool brass door-knob and strained to hear sounds of movement on the other side of the stall wall.

The sound of a zipper echoed off marble-tiled walls.

Viktor turned the knob and stepped out. Once he rounded the wall, he wouldn't have much time. He'd have to make his move right away. The last thing he wanted was for Gregory to see his face.

He moved around the corner on the balls of his feet.

Gregory stood in front of the urinal, hands in front of him. His jacket was unbuttoned and pushed back, held out of the way by his elbows. A hol-stered weapon bulged at his side.

Damn. Viktor's steps faltered. His heart battered his ribs. He'd underestimated Gregory. He should have known the man would carry a gun, even to a youth horse auction.

Viktor forced himself to stay calm. If he was going to do this, he had to move. Catch him while his hands were still busy. Do it, now.

He grabbed Gregory's arm. Yanking it behind the man's back, he shoved him forward. Gregory's body bowed over the urinal. His forehead cracked against marble. Viktor pulled the man's arm high between his shoulder blades and pinned him to the fixture. With his other hand, he brought the pins up behind Gregory's ear, puncturing the skin with the side-by-side tips. "Move, and I will slit your throat."

"Do I look like I'm moving?" Gregory's voice trembled. "My wallet is in my pocket. Take what you want."

"I don't want your money."

"Then, what?"

"What can you tell me about the coup in Rasnovia? Who is behind it?"

"Who's asking?"

"A man you don't want to piss off." He pricked the man's skin deeper. A drop of red trickled into his shirt collar and wicked into the fabric. Any more and he might be able to tell the poke was from a pin and not a knife. But adrenaline changed things. Fear altered perceptions, made threats seem worse than they were. Viktor was banking on it.

"Toma Stanislav. That's what it said in the Houston Chronicle. He's the one you want, not me."

"I'm not talking about the figurehead. I want the source of the money. The soldiers aren't all from Rasnovia."

"I don't know what you mean."

"Mercenaries. Who's paying their bill?"

"I work for a company here in Houston. I don't know anything about Rasnovia."

"I know who you are, Gregory. I know what you made your fortune doing."

"I bring opportunity to underdeveloped countries. That's all I do. I know nothing about mercenaries."

Viktor grimaced. Apparently the pin wasn't doing the job. He needed something to give Gregory a jolt. Make him taste some real fear.

He slipped the pin into his pocket and brought his hand to the man's belt. In one movement, he unsnapped the holster and pulled out a 9 mm Glock. He pressed the barrel behind Gregory's ear. "You respect guns more than knives?"

The man's body trembled. "Listen, I haven't worked in the field in years. I didn't have a hand in what happened in Rasnovia. I swear."

"But you know who did."

He tried to shake his head, his face still pressed against the wall. "I don't know where the money is coming from. My company is on the outside looking in. Someone else horned in on our turf and I'm scrambling to catch up. None of us are very happy about it."

"Who? Who took over your turf? Come on, Gregory. I'm not dumb enough to believe a smart man like you doesn't know his competition."

The man said nothing.

Shoving Gregory hard into the wall, Viktor released his arm and stepped back. He chambered a round and leveled the pistol's barrel on Gregory. "That sound alone would make a smart man think twice about keeping secrets. Are you a smart man, Gregory?"

The man reached down for his open pants.

"Hands on the wall. Now."

He complied, leaving his zipper gaping.

"This is the last time I'm going to ask. Who is behind the coup?"

"I told you. I don't know."

"Then tell me who does."

Silence.

"Now. Your time is up."

Gregory let out a strangled squeak. "The soldiers. I know who they work for."

"Who?"

"You'll let me live?"

"If I like your answer."

"D-Base Corporation. The mercenaries work for D-Base. You find who hired them, and you've found who controls the Rasnovian government now."

D-Base. He should have seen that coming. They called themselves a private security company, but they had more men and better equipment than most countries' armies. And they didn't come cheap. "Lower your hands. Slowly."

Gregory brought his hands down until they hovered at his sides.

"Drop your pants."

"Drop my—"

"Around your ankles."

He slipped his jeans over his hips and let them fall. He stood stock still, bony legs sticking out of white boxers that looked as though they'd been freshly ironed.

"The underwear, too."

He did as he was told, naked from the waist down. And unlikely to be able to pursue or even yell for help until Viktor had a nice head start.

"Lean forward, hands in front of you."

Before he rested his hands on the wall, Viktor was out the door.

KAT HAD NEVER PAID MUCH attention to politics, yet even she had heard of D-Base Corporation in news reports about the work they'd done for the government in Iraq. "So you're saying the U.S. government is behind the coup?"

"I doubt it." Viktor shook his head as they walked across the auction house's parking lot. Night had fallen in the time they'd been in the restaurant, and the weekend's horse sale had drawn to a close. Besides the Volvo Ysabel's cousin had delivered, there were only a few dozen vehicles left in the lot.

"D-Base is a private company. They're based in the United States, but the government is just one of their clients."

Kat let out a breath. Viktor had seemed so excited about what he'd learned in the restaurant. But she didn't see how Gregory's information had changed anything. "So we're back to the same question, aren't we? Who is financing the coup?"

"Yes. But we know a competitor of Gregory's company is responsible. A company that does the same type of work."

"Construction?"

"Heavy construction. Bridges, dams, energy in-frastructure. There aren't too many companies in the world that do that type of work."

She still didn't understand how that narrowed the suspects down very much. "Is that it?"

"No. If D-Base is supplying the soldiers, we have one more way to track the money trail."

"We find who's paying D-Base's bill."

"Right."

"And how do we do that?"

"We don't. Jackson and Ysabel do."

She crossed her arms under her breasts and rubbed the bare skin above her elbows. The air was heavy, moist, a harbinger of a coming storm. "How about us?"

"We get out of town."

Kat scanned the parking lot and the traffic snaking along a highway beyond. She knew he was right. She needed to disappear, to keep Danny safe above all else. But the thought of running again, hiding, waiting for brutal men to find her one day…it made her feel so powerless. So vulnerable. She wanted to take control. She wanted to *do* something. "What about your friend, Deke Norton? Jackson said he would know about all the corporate comings and goings, right? So might he know something about who is competing with Warren Gregory's company? Or what Amal Jabar is doing with his money? Or who hired D-Base?"

Viktor nodded slowly. "He might."

"So let's talk to him."

Viktor gave her a tight-lipped look and shook his head. "We are not going to talk to anyone."

"Why not?" She let the words slide from her lips, not because she didn't know the answer, but because she felt like she was going to jump out of her skin in frustration. She needed to push back at something, anything, but especially Viktor.

"You know why not. You're in danger, and I am supposed to be dead."

"You think Deke Norton will tell people you're alive?"

"Deke can keep a secret. Especially one that important. But if you hadn't noticed, that secret puts people at risk. Being tied to me puts people at risk. I've already put Flint, Akeem and Jackson in a bad position, not to mention you and Daniel. I don't need to add Deke to that list. Not unless I have good reason."

Kat looked down at the pavement under her feet. What a jerk she was. She knew full well the burden Viktor carried, how he felt responsible for protecting everyone, her and Danny, his friends, his country. And yet she was pushing against what she, too, knew was best, just like a petulant teen. "I'm sorry, Viktor. I know we need to get Danny as far from this as we can…as I can. Maybe Flint could talk to Deke Norton. He doesn't even have to tell Deke you're alive."

He tilted his head to the side, considering this for a moment. "That's a good idea. I'll give him a call. But first, we have a baby to pick up from the sitter."

Kat gave him a bittersweet smile. Ironic how normal that sounded. How middle-American. How much like she'd pictured her future to be when she was growing up in the suburbs.

Of course in her visions of the future, she and her man were married and had a house on a cul-de-sac. He wasn't a prince from a war-torn country who was believed to be dead. And they didn't have mercenary soldiers chasing them who were hell-bent on killing them and their baby.

Funny how she'd used to crave more excitement. How she'd longed for more from life. She'd never imagined *more* would be like this.

Yeah, irony was a bitch.

VIKTOR CLAPPED HIS CELL phone shut and listened to the patter of raindrops on the window and the gentle sucking sound of his son trying out the pacifier Ysabel had included in the bundle of clothing and supplies she'd left for them in the car. They had picked up Daniel from Taylor. The whole thing had gone like clockwork and yet a tension headache hovered behind his eyes, growing more solid with each worrisome scenario that played through his mind.

He'd reached Jackson and Ysabel at the D.C. airport. Akeem was still in the air over the Atlantic. And now Taylor was in her car right behind them, both trying to get out of the auction house's parking lot and into the traffic jam on the highway.

An accident ahead, no doubt. Rain fell in glistening ribbons through pools of light at the scene. A highway truck with a flashing signboard parked down the street, warning cars of the upcoming lane closings. From here, Viktor couldn't read the explanation for the slowdown. Not that it mattered. As annoying as the delay was, traffic problems weren't what worried him. No, his mind was occupied by something far worse.

"What's wrong?" Kat asked, as if she was now reading his mind.

He meant to give Kat a smile, but his lips just did a tightening thing that probably looked more like a grimace. "Flint and Lora Leigh. I can't get a hold of them."

"Their phone is dead again?" She sounded a little breathless, similar to how Viktor felt.

"No. It's not dead this time. I reached Lucinda, the housekeeper. She said they arrived at the ranch, but didn't even come into the house. They left right after checking on the horses they bought. And she said someone named Keller had called several times."

"Keller? Didn't Jackson mention an FBI agent named Keller?"

"I don't remember. It's a pretty common name."

He caught the tension in Kat's face in the glow of the overhead streetlight. "You tried Flint's cell?"

"Of course. It just went to voice mail."

"That's strange. I wonder where they went." She glanced at her watch. "Taylor is heading back to the ranch. Maybe she can check up on things."

Viktor glanced at the headlights of Taylor's car in the rearview mirror. He wasn't sold on the idea of asking for Taylor's help. Taylor and her young son had moved into a separate house on the ranch. In light of all that was happening, Flint had confided that he'd wanted to keep her in the main house to ensure her safety. But after Akeem and Taylor had gotten engaged, Viktor could bet that living in the same house as her protective big brother hadn't been ideal. She'd assured them a state-of-the-art alarm system would keep her safe while Akeem was away. But if something had happened to Flint and Lora Leigh, Viktor wasn't sure it was such a good idea for Taylor to be poking around for answers. He'd rather she stay behind her locked door with the alarm system on. "I'll keep calling."

A truck two vehicles ahead inched forward onto the street. A police officer held up a hand, bringing traffic to a stop once again. Beyond the officer, Viktor could see orange cones dotting the street, yellow tape stretched between. "It looks as though one of the lanes is sectioned off."

Kat leaned over the backseat and adjusted something for the baby. "Probably a simple fender bender. And everyone has to gawk as we inch by. Bunch of rubberneckers. I hate that."

Viktor wasn't fond of that particular quirk in human nature, either. But the slowness of the traffic seemed excessive, even for the most ardent of gawkers. "It can't be a simple bent fender that's causing this mess."

Kat settled back into her seat, replaced her safety belt and squinted through the windshield. "There do seem to be a lot of police officers involved."

She was right. In addition to the traffic cop in front of them, the street seemed to be cluttered with uniforms. Two squad cars lined the far curb with more farther down the street. The light bars on their roofs pulsed in the air, making the rain shine red and blue.

Viktor's skull throbbed, as if someone was pounding at his temples with a ball-peen hammer. At least all of the uniforms and squads on the street seemed to be Houston PD. Not that he should assume that made Kat and the baby safe. Until Flint could give him some information about how widespread the corruption in law enforcement was, he'd just as soon not trust anyone with a badge.

The cop motioned to the next car.

Wipers sloshing, Viktor nosed the Volvo forward and took his place at the stop sign. From here, he could see a pickup with the door gaping open. A shadow stained the pavement, darker than rainwater. "Not a fender bender."

"That looks really bad. Like a pedestrian was hit or something." Kat rolled her shoulders back in a half shiver. She pointed to the red neon Francine's

Fine Sirloin sign peeking out from behind the squad cars. "We just crossed this street."

In fact, they had probably only missed this accident by a matter of minutes.

The officer motioned for them to pull out into the street.

Viktor moved his foot from brake to gas, and the Volvo inched forward into the traffic lane. The bright lights all around the accident scene lit the street like a carnival and drilled Viktor's headache deeper into his skull.

The officer raised his hand again, stopping Taylor's car. They moved forward, bit by bit. When they'd finally covered a car length, he let Taylor take her spot behind them.

They drew alongside the truck. Viktor craned his neck, just as he'd condemned others for doing. From the driver's seat, all he could see was the pickup, door open, dome light on, rain soaking into the seat cover.

On the passenger side, Kat had a better view. "Oh, my God."

He'd expected it to be bad. As soon as he'd seen the dark patch spreading in front of the truck, he'd known it was blood. Judging by the tone of Kat's voice, it was one of the most horrific accident scenes she'd ever seen. "Bad?"

She spun in the seat to face Viktor. Her eyes

looked as dark as burned caramel, her pupils dilated despite the pulsing light outside. She pressed her fingers to her lips. "Viktor."

"What is it?"

"This is no accident. No way."

In the backseat, Daniel started to cry.

"Kat, I can't see it from here. What is it?"

A gurgle came from her throat. A strangled sound of fear. "He's dead. On the street. Under that truck."

Blood rushed in his ears. He'd talked to Jackson. Could it be Akeem? Was he not on that plane after all? Or Flint? Could Flint have returned to the auction house? Is that why he wasn't answering his phone?

He felt dizzy. Off balance. "Who, Kat? Who is under the truck?"

"Warren Gregory."

Chapter Nine

"Someone found out Gregory talked to us." Kat's voice sounded tight, a few notes higher than her natural tone.

She was scared, and Viktor couldn't blame her. But it was important they didn't panic now. It was important they chose their next move wisely. "You don't know that."

"What else could have happened? Grown men don't get hit by trucks. Not unless the truck was gunning for him. Or someone pushed him."

Now that was a possibility. "Who? Jabar?"

"He was the last person who was with him." She slapped her palms down on her thighs. "Come on, Viktor. It's too much of a coincidence, isn't it? You just forced him to tell you what he knows, and an hour later he's lying dead in the street?"

He didn't want to jump to conclusions, rush off half cocked. Yet he had to admit, Kat was right. It *was* too much of a coincidence. Far too much.

"Maybe someone at Francine's recognized me. Or Warren figured out who I was, told someone."

Kat's eyes grew even wider. Instead of calming her, he'd frightened her more. "So they know you're alive?"

In the backseat, Daniel's fast, neighing cry grew louder.

"Maybe. Maybe not." He had to calm down, calm her down, calm them all down. He had to think. Ahead the traffic rolled on, painfully slow.

Kat unbuckled her safety belt and ducked over the seat. After a few seconds, Daniel's crying stopped, replaced by the light sound of sucking.

Kat returned to her seat and leaned toward Viktor. "If they know you're alive, they're going to pull out all the stops. For the baby, they could take their time. Send a couple of people. Get him eventually. He couldn't hurt them right away. He wasn't capable of hurting them for years. But if they know you're alive…they're going to send an army."

She was right. They would send an army. At this point, he was the only one who could hurt them. The only one who could rally the citizens of Rasnovia against them. They needed him dead, and they would hit fast and hard.

And if Kat and Daniel were with him, they'd be caught in the crossfire.

His throat tightened. His head felt light as

another dose of adrenaline slammed into his bloodstream.

"How long before they track us down?"

"I don't know. We don't even know if Gregory recognized me, or who he might have told."

"How do we find out?"

He needed someone to ask questions. Someone in the know. Someone right here, right now. Someone like Flint.

Damn.

But wait. Flint wasn't the only one. He had an idea. He hated to drag anyone else into this, but if Gregory had recognized his voice and told someone, he didn't have much choice. "Kat, listen to me."

He kept his eyes on the taillights ahead, but he could feel her focus return to his face.

"I'm going to stop the car. I want you to take Daniel and get into Taylor's car."

"Taylor's car? Why?"

He'd rather not tell her, rather not open his idea to debate. "She said she has a state-of-the-art alarm on her house. I want you to go there and use it. Lock everything, even the windows. Don't open the door until I arrive."

"Where are you going?"

"Just do it, Kat. Please."

She shook her head and crossed her arms over her chest. "I'm not going anywhere until you explain."

She was going to argue with him. He knew it. She wasn't going to understand why he was taking the risk. "I'm going to talk to Deke."

"I thought you said you didn't want to put him in danger."

"I don't." He shook his head. He was breaking his own rules. Risking what he said he'd never risk, yet another friend. He supposed when one was cornered, one could justify anything. But he hated what that said about him.

He looked at Kat. All he knew was that he'd do anything to keep her and the baby safe. Even endanger his friends. At least Deke had enough money, enough power to protect himself. "If Deke has any idea what construction projects are going on in Rasnovia, if he can find out whether Jabar or D-Base or anyone else knows I'm alive, then I can figure out what to do next."

"*We* can figure out what to do. Next and right now." She set her chin. Even with police flashers now backlighting her face, he could see the determined glow in her eyes. "I'll talk to Deke for you. He doesn't have to know you're alive. He doesn't have to get pulled into this at all, and yet we still find out what he knows."

"Not a chance. I want you safe."

"You said yourself Deke will help. So how will I not be safe?"

He didn't have an answer, but that didn't mean he was going to change his position. "What makes you think he'll tell you anything? Especially sensitive information about people he does business with? He doesn't know you."

"I've seen him at the ranch a few times. He probably knows I work at the Diamondback. I can tell him Flint sent me."

It might work. He didn't know. The bottom line was that he didn't want Kat involved. If he could just get a hold of Flint, he could solve this problem. As it was, all he had left was worry. For the baby. For Kat. For his friends.

"How about this? I'll talk to Deke. I'll ask him whatever you want me to ask. And if he doesn't answer, then you can ask him yourself."

He let her idea hang in the air, pulsing like the sound of rubber blades on glass, sweeping away the rain.

"It's settled then." Kat zipped off her seat belt and threw open the car's door. She opened the back door, unfastened the baby's seat from the car and carried it back to Taylor's car.

Viktor wanted to hit the gas, drive off and leave Kat here with Taylor, force her to let him handle it on his own. Let him keep her safe, keep her away from him.

He focused on the bumper of the car in front of

him. He could want until the end of time. But
there was nowhere for him to go.

DEKE NORTON had eight homes sprinkled all over
the country, several in Texas alone, but Kat
couldn't imagine any of them being as spectacu-
lar as this spread in a rural area outside Houston.
From the moment she walked up to the arched
double glass doors and the maid let her into the
two-story foyer with its domed, gilt-edged
ceiling rimmed with mythological figures, she
had trouble catching her breath. Flint's ranch
house was big, but it had a humble, working man
feel to it. A cowboy's home. Viktor's palace,
though grand, had a dignified air, like a museum,
rich in a feeling of history. This place was just
plain ostentatious.

She watched the maid climb one of the twin
suspended staircases to the second level. A
moment later, an attractive man with salt-and-
pepper hair descended and crossed the foyer to
where she stood. His alligator boots drummed on
the inlaid granite and marble floor. His brows
tilted low over concerned gray eyes. He held out
a hand. "I'm sorry, Miss…Edwards is it? Maria
wasn't very clear about the reason for your visit."

"That's because I didn't exactly tell her. I need
to talk to you." She glanced up at the top of the

stairs where the maid dusted the iron balustrade, obviously eavesdropping. "In private, please."

Deke glanced at his watch. Even to Kat's inexperienced eye, the timepiece looked expensive. It probably cost more money than she'd ever made in her life. Deke gestured to a doorway leading left off the foyer. "I should have a few minutes."

"Thank you." She followed his lead, stepping into a room with walls of rich mahogany. A carved wood bar with a granite top lined one wall, complete with the biggest temperature-controlled wine storage rack she'd seen. The place was fancier and more well equipped than any restaurant bar.

"Please, have a seat." He motioned to plush couches nestled in front of a granite fireplace. A gas-log fire crackled behind beveled glass doors, despite the heat outside.

She lowered herself onto one of the sofas. Perching on the edge, she stuffed her hands between her knees so he wouldn't notice their tremble.

"Can I get you something from the bar? Beer? Wine?"

"No, thanks."

"Water?"

Her throat was dry, more from nervousness than thirst. And holding a cool glass might give her something to steady her hands. "Sure. Water would be great. Thanks."

He stepped behind the bar and filled two glasses with ice, then water. As the drink preparing ritual neared a close, the tremor inside her grew. She needed to choose her words carefully. The last thing she wanted was to make him suspicious of the questions she needed to ask.

He sat down and skewered her with sharp eyes. "Have we met before? You look so familiar to me." He handed her a glass.

She wrapped her fingers around the cool, precisely cut crystal. A question that led right into what she needed to ask him. And one she could answer with the truth. "I work for Flint McKade."

"Flint, huh? In what capacity?"

"Horse groom."

His eyebrows arched. "Oh, yes. Of course. I recognize you. But...weren't you expecting?" His gaze flicked down to her belly before returning to her face.

"Yes."

He gave her a wary look. "I trust everything went okay."

"Yes. Everything's fine."

"So was it a boy or a girl?"

It felt strange to be engaging in small talk. The urge to blurt out the questions she came to ask, to get her purpose over with as soon as possible, was overwhelming. "A boy." She lifted the cold water to her lips and took a sip.

"Congratulations. You must be proud."

"I am, thanks."

"That must be something, to have a baby, a little version of yourself, someone who looks to you for everything and loves you without reservation."

The longing note in his voice wasn't lost on Kat. It was too much like the longing she'd felt most of her life. A longing she still struggled with when she was around Viktor. Particularly when he was pushing her away for her own protection. "Danny is wonderful." Her throat felt thick.

"Danny. A good name."

"Thanks."

"You know, I've been very lucky in life, and I have a lot." He gestured dismissively to the grandeur around them. "But I've never been lucky enough to have the thing that's most important of all." He looked at her as if she knew what he was referring to.

Unfortunately she didn't have a clue. "Most important?"

"A family."

She glanced down at his ring finger. Sure enough, it was bare. She couldn't imagine a wealthy and handsome man like him remaining single, if he really wanted a family as he said. Yet men didn't always wear rings. "Are you married?"

"I'm divorced. Twice."

"I'm sorry."

"Me, too. Believe me, if I found the right woman, I'd never let her go. Unfortunately, being from a broken family myself, I guess I don't understand how the whole family thing works. Success in business is far easier to come by."

A pressure centered in her chest, crowding out the nervous tremor. She'd been luckier than Deke, lucky enough to have a precious newborn son, but she understood his longing. She'd come from a broken home, as well. And although she knew both her mom and dad loved her, the frustration of not having a real family, a whole family, was there all the same. She also shared the longing for a mate she could be with forever. A man she could form a true partnership with. A man who would never let her go.

"Are you all right?" His eyebrows slanted downward and he leaned forward with concern.

"I'm fine." She blinked, her vision suddenly misty. "My parents were divorced when I was ten. I know how you feel."

"Like you're forever alone? Forever shut out? Pushed away?" His fingers balled into a fist in his lap, then released, as if he suddenly realized what he'd been doing. "It's so frustrating sometimes."

Not sure she could make her voice work, she simply nodded. Deke really did understand how she felt. More than anyone she'd met. More than Viktor. She leaned back, letting the softness of the sofa cup around her.

"Thank you, Ms. Edwards."

She almost smiled at the title. "Please, call me Kat."

"Thanks, Kat."

"For what?"

"For letting me know things can be different. That someday I might get as lucky as you and your husband."

Her smile faded, any humor swallowed by the void in her chest.

"Now what can I do for you?"

She tried to organize the queries she'd had so carefully planned out when she'd arrived. "I have a few questions about Amal Jabar."

"Amal?" His tone lilted in surprise, but his expression showed only assessment, as if he was trying to read her, figure out the truth behind her words. "Like what?"

"He's been selling his assets the past few months. Then today, he was meeting with Warren Gregory. What kind of business is he doing with Warren Gregory's company?"

He plunked an elbow on the sofa's arm. Bracing

his index finger on his lips and thumb on his chin, he narrowed his eyes.

The nervous shimmer inside her returned. She'd been too forward. Jumped in too fast. Here she'd practiced and practiced a smooth way to ease into the hard questions, and as soon as Deke had focused on her, the first thing she'd done was forget all her plans.

"I don't understand. If Flint has questions about Amal, why didn't he ask me himself? Why send you?"

Kat kept her gaze steady. Viktor had guessed Deke would ask that question. At least she was prepared. "He didn't send me."

"So he doesn't know you're here?"

"Flint doesn't like anyone looking over his shoulder. But he and Lora Leigh, they're my friends. I know something's up with Jabar and Gregory. I saw them planning something at the auction house today, and if they're planning something against Flint, I want to know." She left out the part about seeing Gregory splattered all over a busy street. First things first. If Deke knew about Gregory's horrible death, he might hesitate at answering her other questions.

"Why would you think I know about Amal Jabar's business?"

"I was guessing. Frankly, I didn't know who to

ask. But then I remembered Flint mentioning your name. Something about you knowing all the business deals that go on in Houston." It was thin, but she was hoping the implied flattery would make him overlook the tortured logic.

He nodded. "It's probably just a horse deal."

"Gregory is investing in horses?"

"I've never known Gregory to be a horse person, but I suppose it's possible." Deke leaned back and crossed an ankle over a knee. "Unless…"

She sat straighter. "Unless, what?"

"I know Gregory's company has been doing some work overseas. Jabar might have contacts that are of use to him."

"What kind of business?"

"Heavy construction. Warren works for World Wide Enterprises."

"I've never heard of that company. What are his biggest competitors?"

"There's a lot of competition, particularly with foreign-based corporations overseas. In fact, most of the work Warren Gregory handles is overseas. Particularly Eastern Europe. He just landed a big contract there. I believe it was an oil pipeline. I would suspect that's what Amal is investing in."

An oil pipeline? That was exactly what Viktor had said Warren Gregory had been pushing when they'd met years before. "Where in Eastern Europe?"

He waved away the question. "A small country you probably haven't even heard of."

Kat's heart rate picked up, only this time the rapid beat wasn't caused by nervousness. She'd hoped to get information from Deke, but she hadn't dreamed he'd expose the fact that Gregory was lying. That his company was involved after all. And now he was drawing the line to Rasnovia on his own, without her having to tip her hand. "Are you talking about Rasnovia?"

"You *have* heard of it."

Oh, shoot. She'd forgotten herself. He was probably wondering why a simple horse groom would know about current events in Eastern Europe. "Uh, Flint was considering buying some warmbloods from Rasnovia for his expanded breeding programs."

Deke nodded. "I've seen the Arabians he imported. I wasn't aware he was looking at warm-bloods, too."

Mainly because he wasn't. Flint's bread and butter was in raising quarter horses and thorough-breds. At Akeem's urging, he had imported some stellar Arabians, but he wasn't planning more ex-pansion than that. At least not right now. But if there was anything Kat's personal experience in suburban teenage rebellion had prepared her for, it was telling a good lie. Her mother still didn't know the real story about how she'd gotten her first tattoo. "You know Flint. He's always interested in good horses."

Deke leaned toward her. "If you've heard of Rasnovia, you know about the coup d'état and the resulting violence."

"I saw a story about it."

"The royal family was assassinated, including one of my best friends, Viktor Romanov." He glanced to the side, focusing somewhere right of her elbow, as if struggling to maintain control over his emotions. Silent seconds ticked by. Finally, he rubbed a hand over his face and returned his eyes to hers. "Friend. That doesn't seem adequate, really. Viktor was more like a brother. The only family I have."

A sob built in Kat's chest. Only a few days ago, she'd believed Viktor was dead. She'd felt that desolate emptiness. She'd been drowning in the same feelings she could hear aching in Deke's voice. "He's not really—" She bit the inside of her lip, unsure if she should go on.

Deke leaned toward her. "He's not really what?"

Her mind stuttered. For a moment she groped for words, for thoughts. She and Viktor had decided telling Deke would only be a last resort. She couldn't do it, not yet, even if it would make Deke feel better.

"I'm sorry to interrupt, Deke. Especially at such a sensitive moment." Lawrence McElroy stepped into the room. The lamplight gleamed on his gray hair. His boots drummed on the polished granite and cherry floor. He looked straight at Kat. "Maria said you were in here, and I guess I didn't realize you weren't alone."

"DID MCELROY hear? Did he seem to know what you were talking about?"

"I don't know. Deke tried to help me cover it up, saying we were just wishing an old friend was still around. But I'm not sure McElroy bought it." She looked up at the car's ceiling and shook her head, the longer strands of her hair whipping against her cheeks. "I'm sorry, Viktor. I can't believe I slipped like that. When Deke was talking about how he wished... I guess I just related to some of the things he was saying."

He waved her apology aside. "You did a good job."

"I screwed everything up."

"No, you got the information we needed. The connection between Jabar and Gregory."

She shook her head. "He just said it was possible. He didn't say that he knew they were doing business together. And I didn't get our other questions answered."

"Listen, Deke has his finger on the pulse of business. Believe me, if Deke says it's possible, that's almost as good as someone else saying it's fact."

"So what about McElroy?"

That was another story. Viktor squinted out at the highway, wet pavement stretching over the land like a slick, satin ribbon.

"It's bad, isn't it? If McElroy knows you're alive, I mean."

"I'm not sure." He knew she felt terrible about her slip. And he'd like to soften her self-criticism. But he couldn't lie. Not to Kat. "McElroy and Flint have been rivals for a long time. After Flint bought his thoroughbred stud out from under McElroy's nose, the old man became an outright enemy. I wouldn't put it past him to be neck deep in this mess, just to get back at Flint."

"Flint was the first of The Aggie Four to be attacked. It happened right after the explosion. Before I was even on the ranch."

"The pieces fit."

"So it's Jabar *and* McElroy?"

"They were both at the auction, along with Gregory. Just because we didn't see them together doesn't mean they weren't. And now that we know Gregory lied to us about his company being cut out of the work in Rasnovia, it all seems to fit together." It fit together, all right. And the puzzle added up to no good.

"We know one thing for certain."

"What's that?"

"We have to get you and the baby out of here. Somewhere no one can find you. If McElroy has anything to do with this, and he knows I'm alive, things are about to heat up."

She nodded. No question. No argument. "I can't wait to pick up Danny. I know it's only been a little over an hour, but my arms just ache for him. Physically. Each time I've been away from him. It's the weirdest thing."

Although he didn't have the physical sensation of missing him, Viktor could understand the sentiment. He gave her a smile. "I can't wait to see him, either."

"Viktor?" She placed her hand over his.

He released the wheel and let his fingers close around her soft, warm skin.

"Stay with us in Florida."

"You know I can't, Kat." He wanted to, though. He longed to stay with her, watch Daniel grow up, always be there to keep them safe. He could feel the pull of her words deep in his chest.

"They'll be after you. I'm afraid they'll k—" She dipped her chin and stared down at her lap.

"I'll be fine. Remember, they tried once, and

they failed. What makes you think they won't fail again?" He'd tried to keep his voice light, teasing. But one look at the tears winding down Kat's cheeks told him how badly his attempt at levity had flopped.

She slipped her fingers from his and wiped her cheeks with the palms of her hands.

Returning his focus to the road in front of them, he caught the flash of a white SUV in the rearview mirror. The vehicle followed past one turnoff, then another. It drew closer. The shape of a police light bar stretching across the roof was unmistakable.

His pulse spiked, launching into double time. "Hold on."

"What is it?" Kat twisted in her seat.

"A sheriff's truck. And he seems awfully interested in us."

Chapter Ten

Without looking at Kat, Viktor could see the pallor of her skin, feel her tension fill the car. "McElroy. He called Deputy Stubfield."

"It does seem a little coincidental." In this part of the state, the highways stretched flat and long. Impossible to lose a vehicle that was following. He would have to come up with something creative, and pray he was being paranoid and it was just a deputy out on routine patrol.

He took the next right off the highway. The Volvo was moving too fast and skittered on the gravel. He steered into the slide, and the car righted itself. He pushed the accelerator.

Glancing from road to mirror, he waited for the sheriff's SUV to reach the turn. The path they followed was little more than a ranch road, an anemic trail of gravel through grassy, likely marshy, land. The chances of the truck taking the turn behind them was minuscule.

Unless he really was after them.

A tire hit a hole in the road, jolting the car. Great. All they needed was a flat tire or garbled suspension. Then if it was Stubfield or another deputy on the take in the SUV behind them, it would be over. And fast.

He swerved to miss the next rut. The Volvo handled well, but in this kind of terrain, he'd rather have a pickup.

Kat tightened her grip on the dash, her knuckles showing white. Twisting to look out the back window, she gasped.

Viktor glanced into the mirror. Sure enough, the SUV made the turn. The light bar was flashing now, pulsing red and blue. And if Viktor wasn't imagining things, it was drawing closer.

Viktor brought his attention back to the road. A hole gaped in the gravel ahead. He jerked the wheel to the side. The Volvo swerved and slid, but he managed to keep it on the road.

Bad idea, turning down this road. Sure they now knew for certain the deputy was after them. But they were also stuck on a road that could wash away into the marsh at any moment. Or reach a dead end.

What he wouldn't give to be driving Flint's pickup right about now.

He stomped down hard on the accelerator. Rain

spattered the windshield, making it hard to see. He increased the wipers' speed. The rhythmic swoosh-beat filled the car and blended with the rapid thrum of his pulse.

Behind them, the deputy came closer and closer, closing the gap.

Something glimmered through the rain in front of them. A highway sign. A way out.

Kat pointed at the sign. "Granger Road. Turn left. It should lead us to Flint's ranch."

"And then what? Daniel, Taylor and Christopher. We'd lead him right to them."

"You're right. You're right. I wasn't thinking." Kat pointed in the other direction. "Okay, take the next right. Make it look like we're going back toward the city."

He slowed the car. The gravel tilted upward to the road bed. The tires hit the lip of the pavement. The vehicle jumped in the air, then slammed down on the highway. The steering wheel shuddered in Viktor's hands. Gritting his teeth, he made a screeching turn and stomped down hard on the accelerator.

Behind them, the deputy's SUV took the turn. It seemed barely to slow. Drawing closer.

Viktor pushed the Volvo's accelerator to the floor. It wasn't going to be enough. Their car simply wasn't fast enough. He'd have to figure out another way.

And so far, he was drawing a complete blank.

His chest seized. He didn't dare take his eyes from the road ahead, but he could see Kat with his peripheral vision. If they got caught, it wasn't just him who would pay the price. It was Kat. And he simply couldn't let that happen. No matter what it took. "Kat."

He could feel her eyes rivet to his face.

"We can't outrun him. I—I'm out of ideas. I need your help."

The silence from Kat was deafening. All he could hear was the rasp of his own breath, the thunk of his heart battering his ribs, the tires humming and wipers clapping out a frantic rhythm.

"I know what we can do," she finally said.

KAT'S HEART WOULD BE SOARING if their situation wasn't so dire, if her plan wasn't so risky, if she was sure they'd make it out of this alive.

As it was, she gripped the warmth that had blossomed at Viktor's request and turned all her attention on explaining her impossible plan.

"There's a bayou near here. The stretch that's closest to us isn't very deep, but it's long and there aren't many bridges close by."

He nodded, eyes glued to the road.

This was the part he wasn't going to like. The impossible part. The dangerous part. She tensed, waiting for his reaction. "I think we should drive straight into it."

"What?" He was calmer than she'd expected. Maybe just a sign of how desperate things were.

"There's a lot of grass. It's more marshy than open water. If we hit it at a decent speed, the car should travel a good distance across. We wade the rest of the way."

"And Stubfield, or whoever that is behind us?"

"He'll have to drive pretty far to find a bridge. By the time he reaches the other side, we'll be gone."

"Gone where? Hiking along the highway, waiting for him to pick us up?"

"There's a ranch on the other side. I drove past it almost every day. They had a motorcycle for sale. Maybe we could buy it. Or steal it. Or something. At the very least, we could hide in some of the outbuildings there. No self-respecting rancher is going to let a deputy search through his property without good reason."

"Wait. Have you thought of alligators? There are bound to be some in an area like that."

Alligators. Snakes. Kat shivered deep inside. She might have lived in the Houston area for the past five months, but animals like that still scared the tar out of her.

But they didn't scare her as much as the deputy closing in behind them. And the soldiers he would call once he had them in custody. "I know it's risky. But I don't know how we can lose him any other way. Do you?"

A muscle along his jaw flexed. "You have your safety belt on?"

She stretched the nylon shoulder strap away from her chest and let it snap back. "Check."

"The airbags will probably go off. You'll have to brace yourself for that."

The airbags seemed the least of their problems. "Check."

He nodded slowly, as if trying to find another reason not to do this, another way to warn her of problems to come.

"Let's just do this thing, okay?"

He glanced at her. The look was quick, and the only light on his face was the faint green glow of the dash. "I...thank you, Kat."

"For what?"

"For being a great partner."

Although hearing him say those words were special to her, she already knew. The moment he'd asked her for help, she knew something had shifted between them. Until that moment, she'd never really believed they had a future, no matter how much she'd wanted it, how much she'd longed for it. Now, she felt a glimmer grow inside her. It spread through her chest and suffused her limbs. "We make a good team, don't we?"

He nodded. "A great team."

She focused straight ahead. Long stretches of tall grass flanked the highway on the right. Rain and darkness closed around them, making the far side of the marsh impossible to see. But after driving this road dozens of times on ranch errands, she thought she knew where they were.

She sure as hell hoped so.

She sucked in a breath and waited…waited. If she and Viktor got out of this alive, maybe they had a chance. Maybe they could have the life she'd always wanted. A partnership. A happiness, and yet something more. Something bigger than themselves. A family. A future.

At least that was something she could hold on to. "Okay, turn here and hit the gas."

Chapter Eleven

Viktor swerved off the highway, jammed his foot down on the accelerator and prayed. Next to him, Kat braced herself, one hand seizing the door's arm rest, the other against the dash.

The car bumped and jolted over the highway's shoulder. The steering wheel twisted violently in Viktor's hands. He tightened his grip and plunged on.

He trusted Kat. But this was crazy. A desperate move he'd never have come up with on his own. He just hoped it worked.

It had to.

The car hit the marsh with a skidding, dipping sensation. Grass whipped the hood, spotlighted in headlights. A rumble engulfed them, one sound indistinguishable from the next.

Viktor gritted his teeth. He had to hold the wheel. Had to keep his foot on the gas as long as possible.

Mud sucked at the undercarriage. Tires spun.

Their forward motion began to slow. The car's nose dipped. Sudden. Hard. Viktor's body was thrown forward. The belt cut across his shoulders. A pop exploded in front of him. Something hit his face, then all he could see was white.

He wasn't sure how long he sat there. A strange numbing sensation assaulted the bridge of his nose. A dull pain throbbed through his head and neck.

Kat.

He fought out of his stupor, willing his mind to clear. The white was gone, the airbag already starting to deflate. Kat sat next to him, her hands in a praying posture over her mouth and nose.

"Are you okay?"

"I feel like I was punched."

He could sympathize. "The airbag. We're going to have some nice bruises." He craned his sore neck and peered into the rearview mirror.

The deputy's light bar flashed, the truck stopped on the highway behind. Was he waiting to see if they'd lived? Or was he readying his rifle? Waiting for his chance to shoot and let the alligators take care of the evidence?

The car shifted under them. Cold pooled at his feet. He looked down at the floor under the retreating airbags, under the dash. A smothering scent of moisture and vegetation and mud closed around them. "We're sinking."

Kat nodded. She dropped her hands from her face. Her eyes looked strange in the dark, her nose pink. "We have to get out of here."

"I thought you said it wasn't deep."

"Six feet?"

Maybe not deep for swimming. But six feet was plenty of water to drown in if you were trapped inside a car.

He released his safety belt. Turning to Kat, he clawed the drooping airbag away from her and released her belt, as well. "Try your door."

Kat released the latch and gave it a shove. It didn't move. Viktor tried his door. Same result. No matter how hard he pushed, it wouldn't open. He hit the button to lower the windows. The glass didn't move, either. They were trapped inside the car, the water pressure from outside sealing the doors as solidly as any lock. The water rose over the gas and brake pedals and inched up the floor mat.

Kat grabbed his arm. Her eyes looked clearer now. Her expression sharp. "This isn't just water we're in. It's grass. Probably a lot of stirred up mud. If we both lean on one side of the car, maybe we can free one of the doors enough to open it."

Or maybe they could cause the car to tip, to roll.

Viktor forced himself to stay calm. "It's already starting to tip my way."

Kat scrambled over the console between the

seats and climbed into his lap. He wrapped his arms around her warmth. This close, he could smell the cheap floral fragrance of the motel's shampoo and the sweet scent of her skin even over the odor of living mud.

He drew in a breath of her. "Here we go." He threw both their bodies to the side, pressing against the driver's door, weighing it down.

The car tilted slowly. Cold soaked to his knees as the water ran to his side of the vehicle. The passenger door lifted into the air.

He shifted his weight until he was sitting on the door. The car lay on its side, driver's door down. It felt strange. Off balance. As if it could roll at any moment. They had to get out of here. "Go ahead. I'll give you a boost."

Kat slipped off Viktor's lap and started climbing, using the bucket seats as a ladder upward to the passenger door. She tried the door. This time it moved.

"It's opening, but I can't quite reach it."

Viktor stood on the driver's door. Lowering a shoulder, he slipped under Kat's hip and boosted her.

She pushed the door open.

Gunfire cracked over the marsh.

"Kat! Down!"

Kat ducked back into the car. "He's shooting at us. How—"

He scoured the dark interior of the car. His gaze landed on the suitcase of clothing and supplies Jackson and Ysabel had left for them. "We'll go out together. I can shield you."

"He'll shoot you."

"Not with my body. With the clothing." He nodded at the suitcase. "It won't stop a bullet, but it might make it hard for him to line up his shot."

"Okay." Kat shifted off Viktor's shoulder.

He reached into the back and grabbed the case. Heavy and cumbersome, it took him forever to work it between the seats. Kat held the door open. Muscles straining, Viktor pushed the case out and balanced it on the side of the car.

Another crack shot through the air.

The suitcase jolted in his grasp. He held it fast. "Wait," he said to Kat.

Both of them froze, waiting for another report. A minute passed. Two. Nothing happened. Had the deputy given up? Or was he simply waiting for a clear shot?

"Can you duck down? See where he is?"

Kat stooped and ducked under Viktor's chest. "He's moving. Driving away."

"Okay, climb out. Fast." If he was already moving, on his way to a bridge, they didn't have a lot of time.

Body pressing against Viktor, Kat shuffled

upward and climbed out of the car. As soon as she was free, he released the suitcase and pulled himself up behind her. The case slid off the side of the car and plopped into the tall grass.

Free of the car door, Viktor searched the dark reeds. "Kat?"

"Here." The vegetation swayed and moved. "The water is up to my neck, and from the look of things before I jumped, I'd say we're over halfway across already."

He scanned the area on either side. He agreed. At least they probably wouldn't have to swim. If they could get through this without alligators, all they'd have to worry about was the deputy meeting them on the other side.

He gathered his legs under him and jumped into the dark grass. He plunged into water up to his chest. His shoes sank into thick mud. The water didn't feel as cold as it had in the car, but the heavy odor clogged his throat and made it hard to breathe.

He glanced around him but could see nothing but green and blackness. Blades of grass whipped sharp against his face. "Kat?"

"Here."

Following her voice, he fought back the razor-like blades. She grasped his hand before he saw her. "Don't move," she said. "We have company."

KAT STOOD STILL and gripped Viktor's hand. A long dark shape glided through the water and vegetation not twenty feet away. And even a girl from suburban Chicago could tell what it was.

Alligator.

Her heart pounded so hard she felt like her chest would explode. She wanted to run. To let the panic pressing at the inside of her skull have free rein. To thrash through the weeds and back to the shore. But somewhere deep in the rational part of her mind, she knew that was the worst thing she could do. The way to sure death.

She forced her mind to quiet, to think. They couldn't have gotten this far just to die in a marshy bayou, could they? There had to be a way out.

The shape circled around them and headed back toward the hulk of half-submerged car.

Kat's feet sank deeper and deeper into the muck. Fetid water crept up her neck and lapped at her chin. This was a bad idea. She'd really screwed up this time. Finally Viktor had trusted her. He'd asked for her help. And she'd come up with a desperate, lame-brained idea. An idea so bad, it was about to get them killed.

She wished she could talk to Viktor. Hold him. Ask him to forgive her. But she didn't dare move.

A splash erupted near the Volvo. Another

splash. A shape like a rectangle bobbed on the water in the middle of the commotion.

The suitcase.

Viktor's grip on her hand tightened. "Now." He started moving for the shore.

Kat forced her feet to move, heavy as concrete blocks. The mud sucked at her shoes, her ankles. She plowed through, following in Viktor's wake.

The water grew shallow. The grass thicker. They fought ahead. Finally they reached the shore.

Kat leaned her hands on her knees and tried to catch her breath.

"We've got to hurry."

She nodded and straightened. She wasn't sure how much time they'd burned before the alligator had turned his attention to the suitcase and whatever food smells emanated from the supplies inside. Deputy Stubfield might have already reached the next bridge. He might already have crossed it.

"Which way to the ranch?"

Kat took in their surroundings. Everything looked different at night, especially in the light rain still falling. She hoped she recognized enough. She raised her index finger to point what she thought was south. "That way."

They launched into a fast walk. Reaching the highway, they stayed to the ditch so they wouldn't be spotted. But the dark night wasn't breeched by a single set of headlights.

"You were something back there." Viktor's voice deepened with pride she didn't deserve.

"I almost got us killed."

"It was a pretty risky move."

She shook her head. "I don't know. Maybe you shouldn't have asked for my help. If we'd done what you wanted all along instead of going off on my lame suggestions, we'd probably be halfway to Florida by now."

"And we wouldn't know any of what we know now."

"What do we know? I mean, really?" It seemed hopeless. Like they'd taken risks for nothing.

"We know Warren Gregory's company is building an oil pipeline in Rasnovia. We know D-Base supplied the soldiers that enabled Toma to seize power. We have strong reason to suspect Lawrence McElroy and/or Amal Jabar are involved. Kat, from here it's a matter of following the money trails and seeing who's doing the most political maneuvering."

"The things Akeem and Jackson are tracking."

"Yes."

"So it's all over for us?"

"Yes. We'll pick up Daniel, borrow a vehicle from Flint, and we're on our way to Florida."

She thought of the last two vehicles people had gone out of their way to help them get. Flint's truck had been impounded by the police. And the Volvo… "Won't one of Flint's trucks be traceable?"

"We'll trade it for something else once we're out of Houston."

She felt better. Even her breathing had caught up, and her legs were striding forward in an easy rhythm. Maybe they could get out of this after all. Maybe they could make the whole thing work. "I know one thing."

"What's that?"

"From now on, I'll gladly follow your lead, Viktor. I've had enough of the exciting life."

His chuckle sounded warm and low. He reached for her and took her hand in his. "I don't know if we can go back, Kat. I kind of like us as a team."

Squeezing his fingers, she stopped in her tracks. She pulled him toward her and looping her arms around his neck, she pulled him down to her.

VIKTOR FITTED HIS LIPS OVER Kat's and claimed her. He'd waited so long for this kiss, wanted it so much, but never believed it would happen. She tasted just as he remembered, in the times they'd spent together in America, in the chalet in northern Rasnovia that last night.

She leaned her body against him, soft and warm. The dampness of their clothing made her feel all the closer, like the hot nights when they'd made love, their sweat mingling and making them one.

He wanted to make love with her right now. Taste every part of her, truly meld as one. Join together and never again be apart.

Not yet.

They only had a little farther to go. Pick up their son. Find a car. Drive away. And though he knew their time together would be fleeting even then, if Kat felt up to it, they'd make love in the humid Florida nights until he could be sure she'd be safe...until he had to leave her and fight for his country.

He teased her tongue with his one last time, then ended the kiss. "We have to hurry."

She nodded, and without another word, she resumed her pace. Before long, lights glowed in the distance.

She pointed to their twinkle in the moist night. "That's the ranch I was talking about. When I drove by the other day, they had a sign out by the fence advertising a motorcycle for sale."

Viktor quickened his stride. "Let's hope they haven't sold it already. And that it runs."

They walked along the line of fence. At a gate leading to the main buildings and house, a sign declared they had a Harley Davidson for sale. Like most men, Viktor's heart raced just a little faster at the thought of owning a Harley. Although he certainly had the money to purchase a motorcycle, he always thought the Harley carried with it an image that wasn't entirely appropriate for the leader of Rasnovia. He didn't have to worry about that now.

They hiked up the long driveway. Lights burned in the old ranch house. And parked near a grove of cypress sat the bike.

Viktor stepped alongside it and ran a hand over the black leather seat.

"What can I do you for?" yelled a voice from the house.

Viktor and Kat looked up. A man in his late fifties stood on the porch. The stomach lapping over his belt buckle was the size of a pregnant belly, nine months along.

Viktor summoned his best Texas drawl. "Saw your sign out at the highway. She run?"

He glowered at them and raised a cigarette to his lips. He took a deep drag. "I damn well wouldn't try to sell something that doesn't run." Smoke wafted from his mouth with each word.

Viktor tried to give him what he hoped was a polite smile. "How much do you want for her?"

"Asking twelve thousand."

Viktor mentally calculated what he had left.

Soggy with marsh water and not nearly enough, but maybe it would do. "Will you take ten in cash?"

"Cash?" He peered past them, as if suspecting someone was trying to pull a fast one. "You got it on you?"

"Yeah."

"Come on inside. I'll write you up a bill of sale."

Viktor looked in the direction of the highway, half expecting to see a sheriff's truck barreling toward them. "Not necessary."

"Suit yourself. Don't come whining back to me the first time it don't start."

"No, sir. You don't have to worry about that." He pulled out his money clip. The thick stack of bills was still moist. "If you'll just let me pay you, we'll be on our way."

The man held up a callused hand. "Got to come inside anyway to get the keys." Jamming the cigarette between his lips, he started back toward the house.

"Does she have fuel in her?"

"Filled her up myself," he shouted over his shoulder. Reaching the house, he opened the screen wide and motioned them inside. Kat stepped in, then Viktor. The door snapped shut behind them.

The house's kitchen needed a new floor to replace the worn linoleum, but it was neat. The lemon scent of cleaner hung in the air, mixing with stale smoke. A television blasted dramatic music from the next room.

"Don't step on my clean floor," a woman's voice rang out.

Viktor looked to step backward, but there was nowhere to go.

"Don't mind her," the rancher said. "She'll get over it right quick when she finds out I sold the bike. And for cash to boot. She hates that bike."

Viktor nodded. He sure hoped her hate didn't stem from the machine always breaking down.

"Key's in the family room around the corner." The rancher made short sweeps with his hand, as if pushing them forward.

They turned into the next room, stepping onto gray carpet. A woman sitting on the couch looked up from the blaring television as a crime drama segued into the late news. Her plump lips pinched with suspicion. "Ahh, hello." Her accent was hard. Midwestern, probably. Very different from her husband's easy drawl.

"Mary Ann, these people are interested in the bike."

A wide grin broke over her face, as if suddenly they were her best friends in the world. Just as quickly, she tempered her expression, pressing her mouth into a wary line. "I don't know what he told you, but we can only take cash."

Viktor brandished the money clip, still in his hand. After this purchase, he'd only have a few hundred. Not enough to get Kat and Daniel far enough away undetected. He'd have to ask for more from Flint along with another truck once they reached the ranch.

Provided Flint was okay.

He peeled off the big bills and handed them to the rancher's wife. "I'm afraid they're a little damp."

She counted each bill, slowly, carefully, as if she couldn't quite believe the money was real. Finally she ducked to the side of the room and pulled a set of two keys from a desk drawer. "One key is for the saddle bags. Those are custom. The guy we bought the bike from, he does that kind of thing for a living."

Behind her Viktor could see a scene on television. Flashing red and blue lights. Police tape. A red neon sign proclaiming fine sirloin. The anchor rattled on about the death of prominent businessman, Warren Gregory, and outlined how police were looking into it for signs of foul play.

The picture changed to a shot of his own face.

A jolt traveled through him, tensing every muscle from head to toe. Trying to hear past the rancher's wife's prattle about the superiority of custom saddlebags, he focused on the announcer's words.

"Police are looking for Viktor Romanov, a man who has entered the country illegally."

Viktor nodded at the woman. They had to get out of here, and they had to get out now. Before the rancher realized the man they were talking about was standing in their living room. "Thank you so much." He held out his hand for the keys, but she wasn't finished yet.

She plucked the second key and held it up for his inspection. "And here's the ignition."

Viktor willed her to quit the explanation and drop them into his hand. Beside him, he felt Kat tense. He stole a glance at the rancher who was still staring at the newscast.

"Viktor Romanov, a citizen of a country in Eastern Europe, is currently being called a person of interest, but sources have confirmed he has known ties to terrorists."

Ties to terrorists? Viktor couldn't believe his ears.

The rancher looked from the TV to Viktor. Eyes widening, he went through the comparison again.

Oh, hell.

Viktor gripped Kat's hand and squeezed. He shot his hand out and grabbed the keys dangling from the woman's fingers.

Kat raced for the door, Viktor a half step behind. They skidded across the wet linoleum and slammed out the screen door. Viktor couldn't hear the rancher running behind him, but he didn't dare slow down to find out where the man was. If they were lucky, he was calling 911. If they weren't…they were about to be shot at for the second time tonight.

Kat stumbled. She gripped his hand, regaining her footing. Her palm felt slick in his. Her breathing sounded almost as loud as his own.

They reached the bike. Viktor slung a leg over the seat. Kat clambered on behind him and gripped his waist. He stabbed the key into the ignition. He stomped the clutch and gave it some gas. Just before the bike roared to life, he heard the screen door slam.

He pushed off, rolling forward, giving the accelerator a twist. Tires spun. Gravel flew. They rolled forward and centered over the wheels. Kat gripped him, hard, her body hot and tight to his back.

A sharp pop exploded from behind.

He braced himself for the impact of the bullet. Or worse, for a jolt from Kat behind him. A cry from her lips. But all he heard was the roar of the Harley as they careened down the road.

KAT HELD ON TO VIKTOR. She knew her grip was probably killing him, cutting off his air, but she couldn't bring herself to let up. Her arms ached.

Her shoulders burned. But still she couldn't coax her muscles to relax.

They had almost been shot. Not once, but twice. Her mind was reeling. Adrenaline making her head light, her body shake. All she could think about was staying alive. All she could focus on was getting Danny back in her arms and making him safe.

About a half mile from the ranch, Viktor slowed the bike, the engine taking on a lower growl. He yelled something over his shoulder that she couldn't quite hear. Something about being careful.

Kat was all for that.

Viktor took the next turn and drove through one of the many gates proclaiming their entrance onto the Diamondback Ranch. They drove down a back road, circling around the main house and barns. That summer, Taylor had moved out of the main house and into a separate house on ranch land. No doubt the move gave both Flint and Lora Leigh and Taylor and Akeem some well-deserved privacy. In the short time Kat had known them, both couples had gone through so much.

They all had.

Viktor banked around another turn. Kat moved with the tilt of his body, as if they were one on the motorcycle. The rain had stopped and the night had started to clear. Moonlight peeked through spaces in the black clouds. The humid night fanned her hot cheeks. She willed Viktor to go faster, even though she knew he was already pushing the limits of what was safe. All she could think about was getting to Danny. Holding him in her arms.

They rode past the race track and rounded the barn that housed young thoroughbreds in training. They sped down the long ranch roads, unbroken lines of fence lining either side. Finally she could see Taylor's house and the large weeping willow out front.

Kat sucked in a shuddering breath. Parked under the willow sat a sheriff's SUV.

Chapter Twelve

Viktor cut the Harley's engine and coasted to a stop well before they reached the house.

Daniel was in danger.

The moment he'd seen the deputy's SUV, the world around him had become fragmented. Off kilter. The sensation of Kat's hands holding on to his sides. The whistle of the humid night in his ears. The cold blue tint of moonlight on the truck's light bar. His mind scrambled to make sense of it all.

No wonder the deputy had given up so easily at the marshy bayou. He must have guessed they wouldn't have driven into the water if they had Daniel in the backseat. With Akeem, Jackson and Ysabel out of town and Flint and Lora Leigh who-knew-where, Stubfield had figured out the one person he and Kat would ask to watch their baby. An experienced mother. Taylor McKade.

Kat was off the bike before it stopped. She hit the gravel running.

Viktor swung to the ground, as well. "Kat, wait."

"He's in there. He's found Danny. He's—"

"You can't save him by rushing in the front door."

Her steps faltered.

"He'll just arrest you or kill you. We have to find another way."

She came to a stop and turned to face Viktor. Tears ran down her cheeks, glistening in the moonlight. Her eyes flashed wide. Her hair tangled wild on her head.

Viktor's chest hurt to look at her. "We've got to be smart about this. Too many lives depend on us being smart."

She covered her mouth with a hand. A sob shook her shoulders. Then another.

Viktor strode to meet her.

As he drew near, she raised her eyes. Her head bobbed in a nod. "What are we going to do?"

We. Viktor paused. He didn't want Kat anywhere near the house. He wanted to shelter her away. Protect her. Keep her out of this. But he knew she would never stand for it. They were a team. Even though he wanted her safe, he wouldn't change that. He couldn't. And with her baby inside, Kat wouldn't let him stop her even if he tried.

But that didn't mean she had to go in the house. Not if they could do this another way. He scanned the yard.

"What are you thinking?"

"I want to lay a trap for him."

"A trap? Out here?"

"Yes." His gaze landed on a low brick wall surrounding the portion of the walkway garden near the willow tree. It had been painted white like the house, and it glowed bright in the moonlight emanating from the clearing sky. "I need you to stay by the brick wall there."

She peered up at him. He could see her whole body was shaking. "You're sure? I mean, he's in there with Danny right now. And Taylor and Christopher. He might hurt them."

"I don't think so. As crooked as Stubfield is, I can't see him committing cold-blooded murder."

"Why do you think he's here? To have a tea party?"

"He'll turn them over to the mercenaries. Men who haven't promised to uphold the law." Men who wouldn't flinch when it came to putting a bullet into an infant's brain.

He hadn't said that last line out loud, but judging from Kat's expression, he didn't need to.

Setting her chin, she nodded. "Okay. I stand by the wall. Then what?"

"When he comes out, I need you to draw his attention."

"And you?"

"I'm going to be behind him. On the porch. I'm going to take him out."

Kat drew in a trembling breath, then nodded. "Let's go."

He held up a hand. He had to make sure Kat understood what he was going to do. What her role was. "I need you to let him step off the deck before you do anything."

She nodded. "Got it."

"Let him clear the stairs, then do something to let him know you're there."

"I get it."

"If he draws his weapon or—"

"I can handle it, Viktor."

He looked at her narrowed eyes, the squareness of her shoulders, the jut of her chin. They'd been through so much in the past day, and she'd handled all of it. More than he'd thought possible. More than he'd believed he could handle himself. Looking at her now, he felt like he was seeing a new woman. A different woman. But deep down, he suspected the Kat he could finally see had been there all along. "I know you can handle it."

The smile was so brief, it might have been a trick of the moonlight. But Viktor knew better. He tried to take a breath, his chest simultaneously swelling with pride and aching as if his rib cage had just been cracked open. "All right. Now let's go."

They moved off the road. Running on the strip of grass between gravel and paddock fence, they covered the rest of the distance to the house. The grass muffled their footfalls. The night was quiet. Only the sound of insects coming out after the rain and the occasional snort from a horse in the adjacent paddock broke the stillness. They reached the edge of the fence and stepped into the front yard. Crossing under the willow's wispy branches, Kat grasped his hand and squeezed it.

Viktor squeezed back. He wanted to hold her there, keep her with him, every second precious. Instead, he forced himself to release her fingers and watched her take her position behind the wall.

Turning away, he scanned the darkness along the house. An outdoor patio box sat at the base of the porch. Past conversations with Flint filtered through his mind. A proud uncle bragging about his nephew. Making future plans to teach him to ride a horse. To teach him to hunt. To teach him to hit a ball.

Viktor opened the box's lid. Inside, an aluminum baseball bat gleamed in the light glowing through curtained windows. He grasped the handle and lifted it, the weight compact and balanced in his hand.

According to the news, he was already suspected of terrorism. He might as well add assault of a deputy to the list. Whatever it took, he wasn't going to let the man take his son.

A voice hummed from the house. A man's voice. Viktor stepped to the side of the porch, moving close until he was under the window. Although the pane was closed, he could make out muffled words.

"Tell me where he is and you won't have any trouble." Deputy Stubfield's voice held the commanding tone law officers trained for.

"I don't know what you're after, deputy. Does it look like anyone is here but me?" Taylor's voice. Smaller, quieter, yet filled with a bristling dignity and strength that reminded him of Kat, of Lora Leigh, of Ysabel.

"Hiding a person wanted by the law is a crime, Ms. McKade."

"I'm not hiding anyone."

"But you know where they are."

"Viktor Romanov is dead."

"He's not, and you know it. He's wanted by the law in connection with the death of Warren Gregory."

"That's news to me. I attended his memorial service. And I heard Gregory was hit by a pickup."

"And Katherine Edwards?"

The hair prickled on the back of Viktor's neck. He wanted to beat the man over the head just for saying her name.

"I don't see what any of this has to do with Kat."

"Fine. Stick with that story if you like. I know they're not here. But their baby is another matter."

"I told you—"

"Enough. You can either tell me where the child is, or I can arrest you."

"On what charge?"

"I don't need a charge."

"And I'm not telling you anything."

"Watch yourself, Ms. McKade. With all the contact you've had with men who are under suspicion, you're not going to see your son for a long time."

"Men who are under suspicion? Who? Suspicion of what?"

"Viktor Romanov. Akeem Abdul."

"Akeem?"

"And your brother. The FBI picked up him and his wife today. Or didn't you hear?"

Taylor said nothing. Like Viktor, her mind was no doubt reeling from the revelation. No wonder they hadn't been able to reach Flint and Lora Leigh since their meeting at the auction house. They were in custody. All because they were connected to him.

"I don't believe you. The FBI has no reason to arrest Flint and Lora Leigh."

"I don't care if you believe me or not. Now get a move on."

"I'll only go with you if you call another deputy in."

"What, do you think deputies just drive around looking for something to do?"

"No charge. No backup. This isn't a legal arrest, is it?"

"It's as legal as it needs to be."

"Is someone paying you? Is that it?"

Viktor strained to hear the deputy's answer. Nothing but silence reached him.

"I know you don't get paid enough." Taylor's voice softened with understanding. "Not for the job you do. I don't blame you for taking a little extra on the side. But I can pay you. Just leave me and my son alone."

"Speaking of your son, where is he?"

"Playing with a friend."

Viktor had been a parent for all of a few days, and still that struck him as odd. A young child playing with a friend this late at night? A four-year-old slumber party? He doubted it.

Then where was Christopher?

And where was Daniel?

"Give us the name of the friend. I'll have social services pick him up."

"Over my dead body."

Viktor raised his head over the window's edge. He could see forms, vague shapes through the sheers. Stubfield stood near Taylor. He might even be touching her. Holding her elbow to keep her from twisting away.

"You're going to play it that way? Fine."

A metallic clicking sound reached Viktor's ears. The sound of handcuffs locking.

He tightened his grip on the bat. His stomach jittered. He braced himself, waiting for the door to open.

He could see the faint outline of Kat's head as she crouched behind the brick wall, and he couldn't help but wonder how she was holding up not knowing what was going on. Not knowing that the moment when they had to act was drawing close.

The latch clicked. The door swung inward.

Viktor flattened his back against the side of the house. The way the porch protruded would almost ensure Stubfield wouldn't see him. Not until Viktor had moved up behind him. Not until he raised the bat to strike. And by then, Kat would claim the deputy's attention.

The skitter of light steps reverberated through the planks of the porch followed by the thunk of heavy boots. Stubfield pushed Taylor in front of him. Hands cuffed behind her back, Taylor held her head high, her blond hair catching the glow of the moon.

"Stop. I can pay you. I'm serious. Whatever

you're getting to do this, I'll pay you double to leave us alone."

"You don't have the cash."

"My brother does. Akeem does."

Viktor adjusted his grip on the aluminum. Way to go, Taylor. Keep it up. Not only was she coaxing a confession from Stubfield, she was distracting him, just enough for Viktor to move undetected.

"And as soon as I took it, you'd turn me in for accepting bribes."

"I wouldn't. I swear. Like I said, you deserve more pay than you're getting."

"You're right. I deserve a lot more. Once I find that baby, I'll be getting it."

Viktor gripped the bat until his fingers hurt. What he wouldn't give to take off Stubfield's head right now. He inched closer.

"You can't do this."

"Shut up."

"This is kidnapping."

"I said, shut up. I tried to make this easy for you, but you didn't want that."

Taylor stumbled, going down to her knees.

Viktor stepped close, moving into position. He raised the bat.

"I've had about enough of you. Now get up." Stubfield pulled her up by her cuffs. Holding her arm with one hand, he pulled out his weapon with the other. "Now, are you going to move, or do you want to be shot while trying to escape?"

Viktor checked his swing in midair. Damn, damn, damn. What was he going to do now? If he hit Stubfield with the bat, the man might close his finger on the trigger. He might put a bullet in Taylor even as Viktor laid him out.

Stubfield pushed Taylor toward the car, his gun barrel snug against her ribs.

Viktor's mind scrambled to readjust. He couldn't let the deputy take her. Yet he couldn't risk her getting shot. One second ticked by. Then another. He had to do something. But what?

"You're not taking her anywhere."

Viktor went cold. Kat. Yelling at him. Creating a diversion. Just like they'd planned. But she didn't know what was going on. She couldn't see the gun.

"Let her go," Kat yelled. "Now."

It happened too fast, and yet it seemed like it happened in slow motion.

Stubfield shifted the gun, pointing it at Kat.

Taylor twisted to the side.

Kat's eyes widened.

A gunshot cracked through the air.

Viktor brought the bat down, connecting with the deputy's skull. The aluminum shuddered through his hands.

Chapter Thirteen

Not Kat, no! Oh, God! Viktor's mind screamed. His pulse thundered in his ears. He heard the bat clank to the ground before he knew he'd dropped it.

Think. Don't panic. Think.

Taylor stood beside him. Mouth open, she stared at the ground where Stubfield lay. The 9 mm pistol still in his hand.

"The gun. Taylor, take the gun." He felt the rumble of the words in his throat more than he heard his own voice.

Kat!

"My wrists. I can't."

He moved past Taylor. He knew only a heartbeat had passed. A second, maybe two. But it seemed like minutes since he'd seen Kat's silhouette behind the wall. Hours.

She was down. She was down.

Before he realized what was happening, he was moving, leaving Taylor next to Stubfield. His boot connected with the pistol. It skittered across the stepping stone path and into some flowers. His feet carried him across the stones, through the plants. He jumped over the low wall.

Kat lay on the grass. Something dark marred her shirt. Wicking into the fabric. Spreading. Blood.

No, no, no.

He fell to his knees. The impact shuddered up his legs and landed deep in his chest. *Not Kat. He couldn't lose Kat.*

He grabbed the collar of the shirt and ripped, exposing the wound. It was too dark. All he could see was blood, high on her shoulder, sticky and hot.

She moved. Groaning deep in her throat.

"Hold still, baby. You're going to be okay. Just hold still for a second." His voice cracked and rang tinny in his ears. He yanked his own shirt over his head. Wadding it up, he pressed it over the spot where the blood seemed the thickest.

Kat gasped.

"I'm sorry. I'm so sorry. I have to stop the bleeding."

She gritted her teeth. Her chest heaved, deep and hard. Breathing the pain away, like she had when Daniel was born.

Daniel.

He still didn't know where their baby was. But he couldn't think that far ahead. He had to help

Kat. He had to save her. Whatever happened, he couldn't lose her. He couldn't.

The scene before him blurred. He blinked, trying to clear his vision.

"God, this hurts." Her voice was faint, breathless between breaths.

"You're going to be okay. You are. You have to be." He couldn't believe he'd put Kat in danger like that. He'd known Stubfield had a gun, that he'd be carrying. Even when the deputy had pulled it, Viktor had worried about the danger to Taylor. He hadn't even thought about Kat. What they'd planned. What Viktor himself had asked her to do.

She had to be okay. He couldn't lose her.

"Is it bad? How bad?"

"I don't know. I'm trying to stop the bleeding." Bracing himself for the worst, he pulled the T-shirt away from her wound.

The damage seemed small. A dark slash. Impossible to tell in the dim light. "It's not too bad. No, it's not bad at all." He could tell nothing of the sort, but he would have reassured her no matter what he'd seen. The wound seemed high on the shoulder. Too high to have hit her lungs. Too high to have hit her heart. Unless the bullet had gone in at an angle, it didn't appear bad.

If only he could be certain.

She nodded as if she'd known all along. "Danny?"

His throat went dry. How could he tell her he didn't know about their baby? She would insist he leave her and look. No, she would get up and look herself.

"You're hurt. You have to lay still. We have to call an ambulance."

She shook her head. "No ambulance. The hospital—" She groaned again, the sound deep and heartrending.

"Don't move."

She shook her head again. "The hospital will report a…" Her sentence gave over to breathing.

"I know, Kat. The hospital will report a gunshot wound. The police will find us." Of course she was right, but he didn't care. Not if avoiding a hospital meant that Kat died.

"Danny," Kat repeated, her voice rising. "Viktor, where's Danny?"

He had to tell the truth, then beg her to stay still while he found out more. "I don't—"

She surged upward before he finished the sentence.

He pushed her back to the ground. "You have to stay still."

"You said it yourself, it's not too bad."

"I said it looks like it's not. It's dark. I can't really tell."

"I'm not going to die." Again, she tried to sit up.

He held her down. "If you lose enough blood you will. Now stay put. I'll find him. I promise."

"You're talking about the baby?" Taylor's voice rang clear in the night air.

Viktor looked up from Kat. Taylor stood not five feet away, hands still bound behind her. And yet he'd been so focused on Kat he hadn't even heard her approach. "Where's Daniel?"

"He's fine. He's asleep."

"Where?"

"In the house. He and Christopher are hiding. You don't think I'd let that bastard get our babies, do you?"

A smile played over Kat's pinched lips.

Viktor's chest ached as if the air had been pummeled out of him.

"Bobby Lee Stubfield hasn't moved."

"Is he dead?" Kat's voice wobbled a bit, but it didn't seem to be from remorse. More likely, she was just reacting to the pain.

"I don't think so."

"We need to get out of here." Viktor looked back to Kat. "You stay here. Don't move. I'll get the keys off Stubfield to unlock those cuffs, and Taylor and I will get the children."

"What about Stubfield?" Kat asked.

Viktor would love to leave him there, but he knew they couldn't. "We'll call an ambulance for him, *after* we're out of here. Now don't move. We'll be right back."

Kat said nothing.

"Understand?"

"I won't move. I promise."

"Good." He forced himself to push away from Kat. She looked so helpless, lying there. So vulnerable. And the fact that he'd put her in the situation she was in now, tore at him like talons.

He had to do something. He had to end this mess before Kat or Daniel got hurt.

But how?

Tonight Kat had nearly sacrificed everything. Taylor, too. And Daniel. And Christopher.

This had gone too far. Much too far. In one night, he'd come so close to losing both of them. He couldn't do this anymore. Couldn't put Kat and Danny and his friends in harm's way. Couldn't risk losing everyone who was left that he still cared about. No reason was good enough. No reason so noble as to risk the people he loved most.

It was time for him to sacrifice, as well.

PAIN SHOT THROUGH KAT'S shoulder as she shifted Danny. The wound wasn't bad. Not according to the doctor who'd made a house call to see her, a personal favor called in by Taylor. But the pain whenever she moved her arm or neck? Her vision blurred, a fresh batch of tears springing to her eyes and running down her cheeks.

"Kat! Knock it off. Let me help." Taylor raced across the apartment's living room and leaned over the recliner. She shifted Danny into place at Kat's breast.

The little guy's mouth gaped, searching for his meal, then latched on.

The tingle in Kat's breast morphed into mild pain as her milk let down. She dragged in a couple of breaths and the sensation faded into warmth.

"Good?" Taylor asked.

Kat managed a nod. She was as comfortable as could be expected. "Is Viktor still on the phone with Jackson?"

Taylor nodded. "Judging from what I overheard, Jackson and Ysabel are flying back to Houston tomorrow to tell us how things have gone in D.C."

Viktor had been on the phone with Jackson, off and on, since they'd loaded everyone into Taylor's car and fled from the ranch. Jackson had arranged for them to stay in one of the many apartment complexes he owned in Houston, and Ysabel had seen to it basic furnishings and supplies had been delivered shortly after they'd arrived. Even from halfway across the country, that couple was efficient.

It was good to have such caring friends.

Kat nodded to Taylor, careful not to move her

head too much or too quickly. "I'm sure Viktor will be well versed in any information they've found long before they set foot on Texas soil."

"You can ask him. I'm going to put Christopher to bed."

"Good night, Taylor. And thank you."

"I should thank you. If you two hadn't shown up, who knows what could have happened." She shook her head as she walked down the hallway toward the bathroom where Christopher was brushing his teeth. "I don't know what I was thinking when I opened the door to Deputy Stubfield. I just saw the uniform, and I assumed it was about Flint and Lora Leigh."

Kat knew Taylor was worried about her brother and his wife. And she wished she could reassure Taylor everything would be okay. But she'd be lying. "You did a great job, Taylor. Better than I would have done in that situation."

"I don't know about that. I wish I could have gotten Bobby Lee Stubfield to tell me who's paying him."

Kat wished that, too. "My money's on Lawrence McElroy. It can't be a coincidence that news of Viktor being alive came out right after my slip up at Deke's house."

"*You* did a great job, Kat. Better than I would have done." Taylor's lips pressed into a teasing smile.

202 *Priceless Newborn Prince*

Kat let out a breath. All of them had made mistakes. All of them were in over their heads. "I guess we just have to try to do the best we can. And hope Jackson and Ysabel can learn more about what's going on."

"That's right." Taylor turned her focus to her son.

Kat looked down at her own little prince. Even though she knew a lot rode on the information Jackson and Ysabel had gleaned in the nation's capital, like Taylor, she couldn't seem to focus on that. All she could think about right now was the people hurt in this mess—Flint, Lora Leigh, Taylor and Christopher. But most of all, her thoughts focused on the baby at her breast. Feeding him. Holding him. Loving him.

Nothing like being shot to straighten out your priorities.

She stared down at Danny's little head. He was the most precious thing in the world. She knew that at a level so deep it hurt. She would do everything she could to give him a great life, a life worth living.

They just had to come through this alive.

"ARE YOU SURE YOU want to do this?" Jackson sounded exhausted over the phone.

After all the shipping tycoon had accomplished in the past few hours, Viktor wasn't surprised. "I don't see how I have a choice. Not one I'm willing to make."

"I'm sorry I couldn't find out more about who is paying K Street to push the U.S. to recognize Rasnovia's new government. All I can tell you is that some very important people are pushing it right now. Things are moving forward."

"The outcome is certain?"

"As far as I know, no one in a position of influence is standing against it. At least not on the record. The vote is scheduled to take place in two days."

Viktor closed his eyes. "So maybe there's no point in fighting. No point in risking Kat and the baby. Maybe this is all going to happen no matter what I do."

The idea felt as heavy as a brick in his stomach. From the time he was a child, he'd been raised to lead his country. Every school he attended, every country he visited, every friendship he made, all of it was with an eye to the future. An eye to benefiting Rasnovia. What would he be without that honor, that responsibility, that burden? *Who* would he be?

Yet as life altering and confusing and downright tragic as all of this was, somehow it was liberating at the same time.

He braced himself against the wave of guilt sure to follow that thought. He had no reason to feel guilty. No cause. He'd given his country his all. He'd risked everything that mattered to him, Kat, Daniel, his friends and their families. If the power brokers in Washington were determined to take his country out of his hands, what more could he do? As a man in the United States illegally, as a man wanted by the law, what could he do about any of it? If Jackson's sources were correct, in two days he wouldn't be the leader of Rasnovia any longer. He would be just a man like any other.

And Kat and Daniel would be safe.

He breathed deeply for the first time in months.

"There's always a chance," Jackson said, though the conviction usually present in his voice sounded a bit shaky. "Have you heard from Akeem?"

"No." Taylor had called her fiancé several times after the incident with Deputy Stubfield. But she hadn't been able to get past Akeem's voice mail. And he hadn't called back.

"Maybe he'll have news from his end. Maybe whoever is financing Toma Stanislav and his rebels will have left tracks in Rasnovia."

He knew Jackson was drawing out the possibilities to convince him to reconsider his decision. To give him hope. What his friend didn't realize was that at this moment, in the face of surrender, Viktor felt more hopeful about the future than he had since the palace bombing. "How is Ysabel?"

"Izzy's sleeping. You know, I've heard pregnant

women had to eat for two, but I never knew they had to sleep for two, as well."

Viktor thought back to the hours before Kat had given birth to Daniel. Only days ago, yet so much had happened since then, it seemed like forever. Like Daniel had always been the focus of their lives. Yet in other ways, he felt he hadn't spent any time with her, with their son. Time doing personal things. Special things. Truly living those small moments he would cherish the rest of his life.

Maybe he could make up for that now. If men weren't trying to kill them any longer, if he could straighten things out with the police, maybe they could have a normal life. They'd take the baby for walks. They'd hold hands and talk for hours. They'd watch Kat's Chicago Bears play American football on Sundays and the whole family would take naps together on the couch.

He smiled to himself. "You know, I missed almost all of Kat's pregnancy. But after going through the past few days, I can tell you women having babies are feisty enough for two, as well."

"Are you kidding?" Jackson asked over the line. "They're feisty enough for twenty."

Viktor's smile grew. He couldn't disagree with that. "Take care of her, Jackson."

"I sure will. You, too."

Not quite trusting his voice to come through for

him, he nodded into the phone. He sensed Jackson would know how to interpret the silence.

A voice mumbled something on Jackson's end of the line. The sound became muffled, as if his friend had pulled the phone away from his ear.

"Jackson?"

"I'm here, Viktor. But not for long. It looks like we have visitors."

Viktor tensed at the alarm in his friends voice. Jackson was a man who acted. He didn't waste time getting alarmed, not unless a situation truly warranted it.

"Who's there?"

"From the look of the suits, I'd say it's the FBI."

First Flint and Lora Leigh, now Jackson and Ysabel? "Jackson—"

"Hold tight, friend. I've made the arrangements you asked for, but you might have to fly on this one without me. I hope this all works out the way you planned."

The line went dead, but for a moment, Viktor kept the phone at his ear. "Me, too, Jackson. Me, too."

Chapter Fourteen

Viktor found Kat dozing in a recliner in the apartment's living room. From the look of things, Taylor had retired to one of the bedrooms with her son. He thought he heard the soft lilt of a lullaby coming from down the hall. Although Christopher had seemed proud of his role in protecting Daniel, that didn't change the fact that the poor kid had been through the second big scare in his young life. But if any mom could help her son through it, it was Taylor. When it came to Christopher, she had love and patience to spare.

He only hoped he would make such a good parent.

He stood still and watched Kat sleep, their son at her breast. He had no doubt she would be a good mother. Just watching the gentle but firm way she cradled their son made his heart swell even more.

From the first time he'd met Kat, at a businessman's dinner in the restaurant where she worked, she'd brought a color and spontaneity to his life that he hadn't known existed. At first he'd simply enjoyed being around her, not really believing an American with tattoos had a place in his world of diplomatic dinners and royal functions. He'd been wrong. She was the most noble woman he'd ever known. The bravest. The smartest. And just what an emerging country like Rasnovia needed.

Not that any of that mattered anymore.

She opened a caramel-colored eye, bruises from the air bag purpling a half moon under it. "Hi. What did Jackson say?"

"I'll tell you later." He nodded at Daniel. "Is he asleep?"

She craned her neck to the side and peered at his little face. "Yup. Totally out."

"You want me to put him in his crib?"

She looked at Viktor, then back at the baby, as if she wasn't sure she wanted him to be that far away.

"You don't have to give him up. I can put him to bed whenever you're ready."

"No. Take him. It's a good idea. I'm having a hard enough time with this shoulder. It will be good to give it a rest for a little while."

He glanced at her bandaged shoulder and flinched inwardly. According to the doctor, the bullet had damaged little but skin. Kat had been lucky. But Viktor still felt that any injury she sustained was too much. "I'll bring him back to you any time you want."

She gave him a smile that he felt in his chest. "Thanks."

He picked up his little guy. Cradling the baby powder-scented little body against his shoulder, he carried his son into the closest bedroom and over to the crib. White painted wood and a mattress covered with sheets bearing multi-colored balloons, the crib was the first Daniel had ever had. Viktor would be forever grateful to Ysabel for thinking of that when she'd arranged for furnishings to be delivered to the vacant apartment. She'd be a fantastic mother, too, no doubt.

He laid the baby down on his back and watched him stretch then relax into a deep sleep. Standing there, he had the urge to pick the little body up again. Never let him go. But Daniel needed rest. And Viktor had something very important to ask Kat, and this time he wanted to be able to focus all his energy on getting the answer he wanted.

He forced himself to return to the living room with empty arms.

Kat was watching him, having moved from the recliner to a high-backed couch. "It's hard to quit holding him, isn't it?"

"It's a feeling like no other." He crossed to the couch and sat at Kat's side.

A crooked smile tweaked her lips. Her eyes narrowed. "What is it?"

A jumble of motion centered in his stomach. He was hopeless. Here he was leader of a country, at least for a little while longer. And he had a case of butterflies that would embarrass a school boy.

He pulled in a breath. He had to make sure he said this the right way, used the right words. No political policy speech he'd ever made was as important as the case he was about to make next.

He fumbled with his hands. If only he had a ring. His mother's traditional five-carat diamond passed down to each heir's bride. Or something glitzy from Tiffany's. Or a one-of-a-kind design, modern and brave as Kat herself. Then he could let the ring say the words. He could slip it on her finger and keep watch for the answer in her eyes.

"Why are you looking at me like that?" She tilted her head to the side, then flinched from the pain.

He reached out and smoothed her hair back from her bandaged shoulder. "Are you okay?"

"No. I was shot."

"I heard." He was stalling, and he knew it. But it wasn't cold feet. He knew what he wanted. He had no doubts. He'd wanted Kat for a long time, and for a long time, it had been impossible. Now, in light of what Jackson had learned and the decision he'd made as a result, it could actually happen.

But only if Kat agreed.

"If you don't tell me why you're staring at me like that, I'm going to slug you."

A chuckle erupted low in his throat. It grew, carrying with it all his worry and fear, all his love and hope. It poured forth and mixed with Kat's in a flood of joy over being alive.

"Ow. Don't do that. It hurts to laugh."

"I didn't do anything. You were the one threatening violence."

"It seems my threat didn't work. I wanted you to fess up, not laugh in my face."

"I was laughing with you, not at you."

"I should slug you just for saying that."

If she hadn't been hurt, he would tickle her. Pin her down and kiss her belly until she squirmed. Instead, he leaned down and fitted his lips to hers.

Her arm came up and cupped the back of his neck. Her thumb stroked the fringe of his hair.

Chills broke out over his skin. He delved deeper into her mouth, savoring the heat of her, the taste of her. He breathed her in, lemon and sunshine and baby. Yes, this is what he wanted. This is what he needed. More than life itself.

He pulled back an inch from her lips and looked into those big eyes, the color of sweet caramel. "This is what I want, Kat. What we have."

Her lips curved in a wobbly smile. The wetness

from his kiss made them as shiny as if she were wearing makeup. "Me, too."

"Do you? I mean, if it was possible to be together? To share our lives? Normal lives?"

"It's a dream. A nice dream."

"What if it wasn't a dream?"

A frown dug a tiny crease between her eyebrows. "What do you mean?"

"If we could be together, just regular Americans. Buy a house in Houston. Raise Danny, a brother or sister, maybe get a dog." It was the first time he'd called his son Danny, and he liked the way it felt. American. Normal.

She shot him a mischievous grin. "Depends. Could the house be in Piney Point?"

He knew she was joking about the ritzy Houston neighborhood. "I'm serious, Kat."

"Me, too. But only if you throw in some horses. I've gotten kind of fond of them working at Flint's ranch. I'll even let you teach me how to do dressage."

"Kat, I want you to marry me." It wasn't as eloquent as he wanted. Not as romantic, either. But he held his breath and watched her eyes as his words sank in.

"You asked me this before."

Not the answer he was hoping for. "I'm asking again. But this time I want you to be my partner."

Her eyes filled. She opened them wide as if trying to keep the tears from spilling down her cheeks. "Like I said before, Viktor, it's a dream. A nice dream, but still just a dream. With all that's happening, here, in Rasnovia...with the people after us..."

"What if it didn't have to be just a dream?"

Her eyebrows tilted low in confusion. "Didn't have to? How?"

"Do you love me, Kat?" He thought she did. He'd been pretty sure of it for a long time before her pregnancy, before the explosion, before their lives had changed so much. But suddenly he wasn't so sure. Suddenly he had to hear the words from her lips.

"You know I do."

"I don't. All I know is that I love you. I'd do anything for you."

"I love you, too. It doesn't matter, though."

"It matters more than anything."

"I don't understand."

Of course she didn't. He hadn't told her what was going on. He hadn't explained anything. He took her hand in both of his. "I'm giving up the throne. I'm giving up Rasnovia."

She shook her head. "No. No. You can't."

"The United States is going to recognize the new government."

"They can't do that."

"They can. It's happening. I'm not going to be able to stop it. I'll lose the country."

She paused, as if putting together what exactly that meant. "Then we'll be safe, right?"

He shook his head. "Even if Toma and his rebels get everything they want, I'm still going to be a threat. I'll still be out there, a rallying point for Rasnovians to organize around. And, as my heir, Daniel will be a threat to them, too. They can't afford to let us live."

"So it will never end." Her voice sounded flat, hopeless.

Viktor threaded his fingers through hers. "It will end. I can make it end."

"How?"

"I've been talking to Jackson. He's arranged it."

"What?"

"A press conference."

She looked at him as if she thought he'd lost his mind.

"I'm going to sign away the throne. On television. With an official from the United States administration and one from the new Rasnovian government."

"You're going to endorse the new government?"

"I'm going to end this. The threat to your life. The threat to Daniel's."

"I don't...I don't know how to feel." Tears filled

her eyes, but she looked more confused than touched. "What does it mean? For us?"

"It means we'll be safe. Daniel will grow up safe. We can get that house. That dog. We can have a normal life as Americans."

"Are you okay with that? I mean, you've prepared your whole life to lead your country. Can you give it up just like that?"

"I don't have much of a choice."

"Yes, you do. You could continue to fight."

"A losing cause. Like I said, the U.S. is preparing to recognize the new government. Other countries will follow suit. Holding out only means I'm endangering our son. I can't win this."

"You said all that. But that's not what I'm getting at. Are you okay with it? Here." She tapped his chest with her fingertips.

His throat tightened, and for a moment, he couldn't speak. The fact that she cared enough about his desires, his life's work, to push him to answer that question made him love her even more. "If I can have you and Daniel, if I can know that you're safe, I'll be okay."

Her fingers skimmed up his chest. Her hand cupped around the back of his neck. She guided his head down, his lips hovering above hers. "You can have me, Viktor. You've always had me."

His chest was tight, as if he'd inhaled, but had

yet to let the breath out. She'd given him everything, but it still wasn't enough. He had to ask the question. He had to hear her promise. "Katherine Edwards, will you marry me?"

"Yes."

He brought his lips down those last inches and claimed her for his own.

Chapter Fifteen

Kat reveled in Viktor's kiss. She couldn't get enough of his taste, his scent. For so long, she'd loved him. For so long they had remained apart. By distance. By responsibilities. By his hard-headed need to protect her at all costs. But they were together now. And not only did he trust her as a true partner, now the three of them would be a family.

She pulled him closer, despite the sharp pain in her neck and shoulder. She could hardly believe this would all work out. Despite his promise, despite his proposal, she felt like if she let him go, he'd disappear. That all this really was a dream. She wanted something. Something to make their bond feel real.

She moved her hands down his body. Finding the buckle of his belt, she eased it open.

He pulled his lips away from hers and looked into her eyes. "You were shot. And you just had a baby."

She had to admit she was not in the greatest

shape to be making love. Not just the screaming pain in her shoulder, but the dull soreness between her legs. But she didn't want anything to come between them. Not tonight. Not after all this time. And she had the panicked feeling if she let him go, just for a minute, all that had changed between them in the past day would be gone. That it really was just a figment of her imagination. "I want to feel you inside me. I want to make all this real."

He moved his hands between them and wrapped her fingers in his. "It's real, Kat. The way I feel about you couldn't be more real. But I don't want you in pain. I couldn't bear that. There will be time. After tomorrow's press conference, we'll have all the time in the world."

She smiled, but her eyes filled with tears.

"You don't believe it? That we'll have time to make love? Once you're strong? Once you're no longer in pain? We have a lifetime together."

"I want to believe it. I just…"

"A while ago you told me I needed to trust in you, be a partner."

She nodded. "And you did." She didn't have to think too hard to remember how he'd gone along with her crazy ideas. How together, they'd found a way to survive, at least so far.

"Yes. And it was both the hardest and the best thing I've ever done. But now, you need to trust me. Trust us. Our future." He moved his hand under her shirt, his fingers wisping against the skin of her belly.

"I do trust you. I trust us." Chills prickled over her stomach, her breasts.

"We have a future."

"I know."

He continued to move his hand under her clothes, over her skin. His touch was light, gentle as a warm breeze. And her skin hummed with sensation. He caressed her breasts, massaged her lower back, and when he moved that light touch down over her belly to barely skim the sensitive spot between her legs, her body spasmed.

Pleasure wrapped in pain, tightening every muscle, tingling in her breasts and reaching deep into her womb. Ecstasy took her in wave after wave. And when her pleasure finally abated, she took her turn, touching him, stroking him, his body hard in her fist. When he was spent, they held each other. And then, more than any other time, she knew what it felt like to be loved.

And she wanted to hold on to that feeling for all she was worth.

MORNING CAME TOO EARLY for Kat. After waking in the night to feed Daniel, she and Viktor had slept in each other's arms in the bed alongside the baby's crib. But when the sun streamed through the window blinds and Daniel was again demanding milk, somewhere in the back of her subconscious, she knew the comfort of their night together was nearing a close.

A knock sounded on the bedroom door.

"A minute." Viktor thrust himself from the bed where Kat was nursing the baby. He pulled on a pair of clean pants Ysabel had included with the other supplies.

In the daylight, Kat could see the scar slicing across his stomach and the angry red burn marks on his arms. Just some of the scars he'd endured for his country. Just a small portion of the price he'd been willing to pay.

He opened the door. Taylor stood in the hall, holding her cell phone aloft. "It's Akeem. He has news."

A chill moved over Kat's skin and settled into her bones. She didn't have to be psychic to see it was bad news. The tightness at the edges of Taylor's mouth, the bleak tone of her voice, all of it said this would not be a pleasant call.

Kat focused on Viktor. Last night he'd told her of his plans to endorse the new government of Rasnovia. To give up his country and his dreams of ushering it into democracy. He'd promised to give up the throne, to make Danny and her safe, to join with them as a family. She knew he would keep those promises.

She just wasn't sure how much the promises would cost.

"Thanks, Taylor." Face unreadable, Viktor held out his hand for the phone and glanced back at Kat. "I'll take the call out here so I won't disturb you."

It would be so easy for her to let them walk out. Let them talk in the next room where she didn't have to hear. Where she didn't have to know what bad news Akeem had to report. All she had to do was say nothing, and she could stay blissfully happy. Blissfully ignorant. "I want to hear the call."

Viktor shook his head. "You look tired, Kat. You should rest. And the baby—"

"I have to know what's going on." A tremor nudged up under her rib cage. What was she doing? From every indication Taylor had given, things were bad in Rasnovia. But that wasn't her problem. In a few hours, it wouldn't be Viktor's problem, either. All she had to do was let them go. Do nothing.

Hide her head in the sand.

And why shouldn't she? She and Viktor deserved a break. They deserved to be happy. They deserved to enjoy their son and each other without looking over their shoulders every moment, waiting for the next bullet to strike, waiting for one of them to die.

She'd wanted a family her whole life. A complete family. And now she and Viktor would have that. Now she could give that gift to her son.

"Really, Kat. I'll fill you in later. I promise."

She closed her eyes. She wanted to let things go. She needed to.

But she couldn't. "I have to hear."

"Kat—"

"Please, Viktor. I need to know. How can I help you through this if I don't know what's going on?"

He let out a heavy breath. Walking past Taylor, he left the bedroom. When he returned, he held the prepaid cell phone they had gotten last night to replace the one they'd ruined in the marsh. A couple of minutes later, he'd set the phone so the conversation could go three ways. He handed the second phone to Kat.

"Thanks," Kat said.

"Remember, Kat. I can't win. No matter what Akeem has found out, it's not going to change anything." Viktor brought Taylor's cell phone to his ear. "Akeem. Kat is on with us. She needs to hear this, too."

"Hello, Kat." Akeem's voice sounded strangely close for being halfway around the world. "I hope you're well."

Last night she'd been well, better than she'd been for a long time. Since the sun had risen this morning, she was not so sure. "Thanks, Akeem. We're doing okay."

"Go ahead, Akeem."

"First, I can confirm that it is D-Base who is providing the army to Stanislov's new administration. Also there are plans to bring an oil pipeline through the country, among other things."

"So World Wide Enterprises is in this up to their necks."

Kat recognized the name of the company Warren Gregory had worked for.

"Not World Wide. At least they're not directly involved."

"Then who?"

"A company called Trifecta Corp. It could be a subsidiary of WWE. A way to keep their hands clean."

"Why do you think that?"

"Because Trifecta is based in the Caymans. There's no way for any of us to track who really owns the company."

"So they're a front company."

"Yes. And I can't tell you who they're fronting for. At least not yet."

"The name is interesting," said Viktor. "Trifecta. As in picking the trifecta at the racetrack."

Kat sat up, trying to ignore the sting in her shoulder. "Lawrence McElroy. He has race horses."

"Exactly." Viktor nodded to her. "What else do you have, Akeem?"

Akeem didn't answer for several seconds, his silence making Kat afraid to hear what was coming next.

"Are you sitting down, Viktor?" he finally asked.

"Yes." Viktor remained standing. Kat could see his chest rise and fall, as if he was taking one last breath before going under. "Go ahead."

"It's Ilona Vargha." Akeem's voice grew hushed.

A chill crept up Kat's spine. She knew the name. The servant who worked in the palace. The woman who'd taken Viktor in after the explosion. The one who'd saved Viktor's life. "What about her?"

"She was arrested."

"Arrested." A muscle twitched along his jawline. "Where are they holding her?"

"Viktor," Akeem said, his voice carrying a warning note. "She was executed. It happened the day before I arrived. I'm sorry."

Viktor stared straight ahead, his face showing no thoughts, no emotion. As if he was carved from wood. "What about her family?"

"The oldest son was arrested with her. He was put in a prison in the north. I don't know if he's alive or not."

"And the daughters? The youngest son?"

"The daughters are missing."

Kat felt cold inside. She knew what girls missing could mean in a war-torn country like Rasnovia. With no rule of law, no way to protect the innocent, the powerless…she shuddered.

Akeem went on. "The youngest son was put in an orphanage. There are a lot of orphanages now. Some as a result of the new government trying to establish its power, some from the rest of the country fighting back. They're all over, cobbled together to give some care to the children left behind." Akeem's voice cracked.

Tears pressed at the back of Kat's eyes. "Why? Why was Ilona executed?"

"According to my source, she was caught forwarding e-mails from the palace computers, e-mails that suggested the mercenary forces securing Rasnovia didn't work for the rebels directly, but for an American corporation."

Kat jolted up in bed. Pain sliced through her shoulder. Her stomach lurched. She gritted her teeth to keep from being sick. "Trifecta, and whoever owns it."

"Right. She forwarded the e-mails to her home computer, but that was seized at the time of her arrest."

Viktor closed his eyes and leaned back against the wall. He looked as sick as Kat felt.

Tears swamped Kat's eyes and trickled down

her cheeks. She let them come. Less than an hour ago, she was happier than she had ever been in her life. She thought she had it all, as tenuous as she feared it might be. And now?

A sob stuck in her throat and shook her shoulders. She opened herself to the pain, welcomed it, embraced it. Her dream of a family was right in front of her, close enough to grab with both hands. But she knew she couldn't claim it. Not when it meant asking others to pay a price she wasn't willing to pay. Not without losing her soul.

Or letting Viktor lose his.

Chapter Sixteen

"Viktor."

Viktor closed the cell phone and avoided Kat's gaze. He could tell by the tone in her voice that he didn't want to have this conversation. "Nothing that Akeem told us changes anything, Kat."

"How can you say that?"

Daniel squirmed in Kat's arms, no doubt reacting to the edge in her voice.

"If we knew who owned Trifecta, if we could prove they were financing the overthrow of a sovereign government—"

"I don't care about any of that."

"That is what we have to care about, Kat. Knowing those things, proving them, is the only way we can change anything."

"You can't go to the press conference today." Her chest hiccupped in a sob. "You can't endorse the people who killed Ilona, who did God-knows-what to her children."

He closed his eyes and leaned back against the doorjamb. At Akeem's words, a knife-sharp pain had lodged between his ribs and refused to let up. Ilona had risked her family for him. She'd given her life trying to help her country. He knew all those things. But what Kat was suggesting…

He shook his head. "I've spent my whole life fighting for my country. I've given up everything. But that's not the choice anymore. The fight for Rasnovia is all but over. Thinking we can overcome an enemy when we don't even understand who that enemy is? That's naive. The choice isn't between working for Rasnovia and endorsing Ilona's murderers."

"What is it then?"

"It's between keeping our son safe and losing him."

Kat leaned away from him, as if his words were a physical slap. She smoothed her fingertips over Daniel's wispy hair, soothing him. "We won't let that happen."

"How can you say that? You have a bullet hole in your shoulder."

"It's a scratch."

"Not hardly. A few inches to the right, and you wouldn't be here right now. And Daniel? Our son was one brave four-year-old away from being killed."

"Ilona died. One son is in prison. Her daughters…"

Viktor was grateful she didn't finish the sentence. He knew what was happening to those sweet little girls. What always happened in war. The innocent paid. The women suffered. The children died or were left behind. That those things were happening to his people—to people he personally knew, to people who had saved his life—it was unbearable.

"But how can we raise our son knowing we let this happen? That we could have saved other children but we chose to let them suffer instead?"

"We didn't let anything happen, Kat."

"If you quit fighting, you will. If I pretend nothing is wrong and go along with you, I will." She drew in a shuddering breath. "I know you've spent your life trying to make your country a better place, while I was spending money at the mall. I know I have no right to question you. I know. But if we give up while there's still a chance, I don't know how we can look at ourselves in the mirror. If we leave the world to people who would make children orphans and do unspeakable things to two girls, I don't know how we can look our son in the eye."

He couldn't hear this. What Kat was asking him to do was impossible. What she was asking him to risk, he couldn't bear to lose.

He shoved upright on his feet and turned toward the door. He had to take a shower. He had to get ready. The press conference Jackson had scheduled would take place in under two hours.

"Viktor? What are you going to do?"

He couldn't look at her. "The best I can."

"You can't endorse the new government. Not after this."

"I can't risk your life. I can't risk my son."

"You're scared, but—"

"Bloody right, I'm scared. Aren't you?"

"Of course, but it's not that simple. If these people are allowed to do whatever they want, if no one fights them, what kind of a world is Danny going to grow up in? What kind of a future is he going to have? What future are the children just like him, the children of Rasnovia going to have?"

Viktor had been asking himself those same questions. He hadn't come up with an answer. And he wasn't sure there was one to be had. "I can't risk losing him, Kat. I can't risk losing you. Not anymore. You're asking the impossible."

"If you do this, you'll lose us anyway, Viktor."

"What are you saying?"

"I can't go along with it. I can't be part of it."

So that's the way it was. There would be no happy ending. No home and dog. No special family times. "You're sure?"

Tears glistened on Kat's cheeks. She nodded her head.

"I can't live with it. I don't think you can, either."

He felt numb. Dead inside. He wasn't surprised Kat would make this decision. He'd always known she had a warrior inside her. A strong sense of justice. She would have made a wonderful queen. "At least you'll be safe."

"What good does it do to be safe if it means giving up everything you are?"

He couldn't answer that. He didn't even know how to try. "I'll do what I must."

KAT YANKED HER JEANS over her hips, pulling one side, then the other alternately with the same hand. Leaning against the bedroom doorjamb, she pinched the denim against the frame, holding it still while she slipped the button home. Her shoulder ached like crazy, but it was nothing next to the ache of her heart.

She'd replayed every word that had passed between them this morning. But no matter how she obsessed, the result never changed. Her dreams of a real family were gone. Somewhere deep inside, she'd known it was impossible. And in the end, she'd been proven right.

She listened to the sounds of Taylor bustling

around the living room, getting ready to venture out for groceries so they could hunker down in their little fortress until they were sure Viktor's plan had worked. She and Christopher would be leaving soon, and when they did, Kat would be ready.

She moved to the crib and looked down at Danny. He lay perfectly still, arms flailed out to the side, legs splayed open, curving inward like a cowboy who'd ridden too many fences.

She could understand Viktor's fear of losing him. She was scared out of her mind. And even if she took him far away, even if they hid, there was still the risk the mercenary soldiers would find them like they'd found her at Flint's ranch.

But when she looked at him, she also saw a little boy she'd never met. A little boy without a mother. A little boy who was scared. A little boy who needed his prince to give him and his country a future.

If she left. If she took Danny far away, Viktor could do what he was born to do. He could fight for his country's freedom, what she and Danny were preventing him from doing now.

And as a result, she could save him, as well.

She groped in her baby bag and pulled out a pad and pen. Leaving a note was a hell of a way to say goodbye, but if she said it in person, he'd never let them go. No, this was for the best. For Viktor. For his country. And for the future, especially her son's.

VIKTOR WASN'T READY for the crowd of reporters jamming the suburban Houston courthouse briefing room. After catching his face on the rancher's television, he'd known his whereabouts were a big story. But he hadn't had a clue how big. Not only was every news service and television station in the area present, but federal, state and local law enforcement was there, as well. An FBI agent named Ross Keller had even talked to him briefly. All questions, no answers. Viktor had resolved to give him nothing, until he was sure he wasn't just another lawman on the take.

But regardless if they were honest or not, he had a bad feeling they weren't going to let him walk away a free man.

He scanned the crowd. Rasnovia had never received as much attention from the United States as it was getting right now. Too bad it wasn't happening under better circumstances. Too bad it couldn't bring something positive to his country.

The absence of the other members of The Aggie Four inspired a heavy feeling deep in his gut. Viktor still didn't know what the FBI had done with Flint and Lora Leigh. And he hadn't heard word one from Jackson or Ysabel since their phone call last night. He knew only Akeem to be safe, if you could call being stuck in a war-torn country safe. At least Taylor and Kat and their sons were protected.

"Viktor."

He turned in the direction of the familiar voice.

Deke Norton stood in the other doorway leading into the room. The fluorescent lights sparkled off his salt-and-pepper hair. Maybe a little more salt than the last time Viktor had seen him, but other than that, he looked like the same sharply dressed, fit man.

He strode across the room. "You really are alive." He put his arms around Viktor and clapped him on the shoulder.

"Sorry I couldn't tell you before, Deke. Things have been…difficult. I didn't want to drag you into this mess."

Deke pressed his lips into a hard line. Apparently he was about as happy as Flint and Jackson that Viktor had kept the truth from him. "You know you've always been like family to me, Viktor. Even if you and the other three like to keep me at arm's length." He smiled, as if in an attempt to dissipate the hurt and anger pulsing from his voice.

"I apologize, Deke. I've been wrong about a lot of things." Although if he had things to do over, he'd only go to greater lengths to protect those he cared about. The Aggie Four. Kat. Daniel. And although he couldn't live the past over again, he could do his best to fix things now.

"Forget it." Deke waved a hand, as if sweeping it all away, but the stiffness in his movement suggested he was likely to remember the slight for a long time.

Not that Viktor could blame him.

Deke glanced at the crowd outside the room. His smile faded. "Let me help you now."

Viktor nodded, although he couldn't think of what Deke could do.

"I've seen the stories on the news, and I don't believe you had anything to do with Warren Gregory's death. But that's not what I'm hearing from the Houston PD. And I heard the sheriff's department wants to charge you for an assault on a deputy? What is that about?"

"Deputy Stubfield." A charge he actually was guilty of, but he didn't figure telling Deke that was the best move. Better to avoid the whole topic. He'd have enough trouble answering to the law after this press conference was over. "And the FBI? What have you heard from them?"

"They suspect you of terrorism. Namely having a connection to that shipment of Rasnovian saddles on one of Jackson Champion's ships. The one that ended up being rather…explosive."

"Great."

"Ridiculous charges, I know. That's why I've brought a team of lawyers with me. And if things go right, you'll be able to walk out of here today, despite all this BS."

Viktor gave Deke a genuine smile. He had to admit that from the time he and the other members of The Aggie Four had first met Deke shortly after college, he'd felt a hint of resentment from the man. Over the years that feeling had ebbed and flowed, but it had never completely gone away. But today, Viktor felt stupid…and humbled. Deke had come through for him when he'd needed help most. All of the friends he'd made through Texas A&M had. Far more than he'd ever come through for them. "You know what I'm about to do?"

"I can guess."

"Any thoughts?" He'd always been able to rely on Deke for advice. And looking back, he probably should have taken it more often.

"I wouldn't presume to know what it's like to rule a country. Do whatever you think is right, and I'll back you up."

Viktor nodded. It was good to know Deke had his back. It would be even better to know what was right.

If these people are allowed to do whatever they want, if no one fights them, what kind of a world is Danny going to grow up in?

He tried to push Kat's words from his mind. It was too much to ask of him. Too much to expect him to give. Wasn't it?

"I think they're ready for you, Viktor. Good luck. I'll have a car waiting for you after my lawyers do their thing." Deke went out the door he'd come in, avoiding the crush out front.

Viktor couldn't blame him for that, either. Facing the spotlight was Viktor's job. Viktor's responsibility. And one he would not shirk.

He stepped out of the room and walked up in front of the cameras. To one side of a small podium in the center stood a man he recognized from his own government in Rasnovia. A man now serving Toma Stanislov and his new authoritarian regime. On the other stood a large man with three chins lapping down over his red tie. The representative of the U.S. government's state department.

Dipping his hand into his pocket, Viktor drew out the note card he'd scrawled his thoughts on before he'd left the Houston apartment. He let his eyes skim over the speech. Short. Sweet. To the point. The death of Rasnovia's dream of democracy.

He felt like he was going to be sick.

The camera lights came on, the glare blinding.

The FBI agent who had been waiting for Viktor at the courthouse this morning stepped behind the podium and outlined the legal situation for the press. The man with multiple chins followed up with the administration's role in bringing peace to Rasnovia.

Peace. But at what price?

The man's voice droned in Viktor's ear. As much as he tried to focus on the words, he couldn't. As much as he wanted to convince himself he was really here, really about to give his country over to a handful of rebels and an army bought and paid for by some unknown corporation, his mind wouldn't accept it.

He glanced through the crowd again. He missed seeing Flint, Akeem and Jackson. He even missed seeing Deke.

But the one he wanted here most was Kat.

What good does it do to be safe if it means giving up everything you are?

He couldn't argue with her when she'd said those words…couldn't argue with her because she was right. He'd never run from a fight before. Not when the stakes were so high. His country's freedom. His country's future. A future that tied Rasnovia, that tied him, that tied his son to the rest of the world.

Kat had seen that. Flint and Akeem and Jackson

had seen that. And if he was being honest, he'd seen it, too.

He was just too afraid to recognize it.

The room fell silent, and he realized the man from the state department had ended his speech. They were all waiting for his pronouncement. His declaration of surrender to Toma's government. His choice of safety over what he knew was right.

His father would be ashamed.

He stepped to the podium. The television cameras stared at him, their bright lights hot on his face. Back in the Houston apartment, Kat was watching. And he talked to her as he stared down those bright lights. "I wasn't born in Rasnovia, but in London. I learned of my country through stories and songs, and was raised to love it more than life itself. When I was a teen, my father was assassinated for trying to break his country away from the rule of the Soviet Union. It was his life's challenge to see our country liberated. It was his life's dream. And when Rasnovia won its independence, my father smiled down from above."

Toma's man cleared his throat at the side of the podium. Flashes popped from the newspaper reporters at the back of the room.

"It has been my challenge to bring Rasnovia into the future. The future my people have chosen is one of democracy and liberty, and it is my dream to usher in that new era."

Viktor steeled himself for the most difficult part of what he had to say. The part that pained him more than any physical scar. "Five months ago, my mother and the rest of my family died in a palace explosion on Rasnovian Independence Day. Many thought I had died in that explosion, as well, and control of the government was seized by a faction of my administration. This faction is being financed by a multinational corporation based right here in America, a corporation who desires to claim my country to add to their profit."

A gasp rose from the crowd. Suddenly the press exploded in a flurry of PDAs and cell phones.

Viktor raised his voice over the din. "I stand here today to promise I will not hand my country over to these people who seek profit at the expense of freedom. Like my father before me and I hope my son after me, I will stand up to these forces."

Tears blurred his eyes, but he didn't wipe them away. "I am only one man fighting an unknown enemy. But the important thing is that I will fight. I will fight for liberty. I will fight for democracy. I will make good on my promises and deliver freedom to my people or I will die trying. My question to you, America, is will you stand up with me?"

KAT STARED AT THE STILL PICTURE of Viktor on the television set, as a reporter tried his best to sum up the history that had just taken place. Her whole body was shaking. With fear. With pride. But mostly with love.

She had been about ready to walk out the door when she realized it was time. At first she told herself watching Viktor's speech was senseless, a way to hold on to a fantasy that was already dead. He'd looked pale in the television lights. Tired. Troubled. And before he'd started talking, she'd nearly snapped the thing off.

She was glad she hadn't.

The man who'd spoken about challenges and dreams, tragedies and noble fights was the man she'd fallen in love with, the man she'd seen inside him, even when he hadn't been able to see himself.

The leader of Rasnovia.

The father of her baby.

She picked up Danny with shaking hands, propped the back of his head against her chest and pointed him at the TV. "That's your daddy, little guy. A great man. A brave man. A man who loves you more than anything."

Tears dripped from her chin onto his soft hair. She knew he couldn't see the image on the screen. She knew even more that he wouldn't remember this moment. But she would tell him about it always. And when all this was over, and they were out of hiding, Danny would know his daddy's greatness firsthand.

The door buzzer cut off her thoughts.

She set Danny back on the blanket she'd thrown on the floor and walked to the security console next to the apartment door. Could Taylor have forgotten her key? The press conference had been live, so there was no way Viktor was at the door. With his legal troubles, most likely he wouldn't return to the apartment for a long time.

Something she could work on finding help to straighten out.

She picked up the security phone and turned on the video monitor. A familiar smile graced the screen, and she couldn't help returning it, even though the camera's image only went one way.

Today, all her prayers were being answered. Help was on the way.

Chapter Seventeen

By the time Viktor was able to walk away from the courthouse, the sun had long since set. Without Deke's crack team of attorneys, he was sure he'd have been locked up, maybe for a very long time. Instead, after signing his life away and agreeing to continue to cooperate with authorities, he was a free man. At least for the time being.

He couldn't wait to see Kat.

When he'd left her this morning, he'd felt sick inside. Of all the things he'd faced, her disappointment in him had stung the most. And even though they would have to be apart and she and the baby would have to be in hiding far away, at least he would know she was proud.

And most of all, safe.

The limo Deke had sent for him turned onto the street where the apartment was located. When he hadn't been answering police questions, he'd spent the time figuring out what to do next. And even though he hadn't run his ideas by Kat, he hoped she'd agree. With Deke's car and driver at his disposal, there was no need for him to drive Kat to Florida. And as much as he wanted to be with her and Daniel, even for a day or two, they'd be safer taking the trip on their own.

Of course, he still had to sell that plan.

The limo made it through two stoplights on green and came to a halt in front of Jackson's apartment building.

"I'll be inside a little while."

The chauffeur nodded. "Very good, sir."

He climbed out of the car and bounded onto the sidewalk. He wished they had more time. Time to talk. To kiss and make up. Especially to make up. Their touching games last night had only served to stoke his desire, not satisfy it. If Kat said she wanted to make love tonight before she left, Viktor didn't know if he could refuse.

Maybe it would work if he was extra gentle.

He reached the door and stood in front of the security camera. Picking up the phone, he typed in the apartment number and looked straight into the lens.

The upstairs security phone picked up on the first ring. "Viktor. I'm so glad you're here."

Not Kat's voice. "Taylor?"

"Is Kat with you?"

"Is Kat… What do you mean?"

"She's not here, Viktor. Christopher and I left to get some groceries. When we got back, she was gone. I was worried, but I didn't have anyone to call." The panicked rush of her words faltered. "I was hoping she decided to go to the courthouse. I was hoping she was with you."

"She's not with me, Taylor." His throat constricted. His chest felt heavy, like his lungs were filled with lead. "Buzz me in."

The buzzer rang, and he opened the door.

This morning, the lift hadn't seemed slow. Tonight it seemed to take forever. He watched the lights flash over the door, lighting up one by one. He willed the car to move faster. Finally the bell sounded and the door slid open.

Taylor was leaning out of the apartment door and into the hall. "I found something…in her room…but it doesn't make any sense."

He ran the few steps to the apartment door and followed Taylor inside. She led him to the bedroom he and Kat had shared the night before. She crossed to the bed, picked up a slip of paper and thrust it toward him.

He studied the paper and read the deft lines written in Kat's hand.

Dear Viktor—

I know this is not the way to say goodbye, but after this morning, we both know this is coming. I hope you'll reconsider your decision before you go in front of the cameras. I hope you'll live up to the man I know you are inside. I'm afraid if you go ahead with your plan, you'll regret it the rest of your life. I can't be part of that, and neither can Daniel. I'll love you always, and Danny will know his father, if only through my stories.

Love, Kat.

Viktor balled the paper in his hand. So she hadn't seen the press conference after all. It had been only his imagination that had caused him to sense her, watching, loving him through the television camera.

But while that obvious fact made him feel desolate inside, that wasn't what worried him most. When she'd left with Daniel, she had believed they would be safe. And if he'd gone through with his plan, they would be.

The problem was, he hadn't gone through with his plan.

He spun on his heel and rushed past Taylor and out the door.

"Wait." Taylor ran behind him. "There's more."

He stopped in his tracks.

In the living room, Christopher sat in front of

the television, watching a show that featured animals that danced and sang and played pretend in their backyard.

Taylor motioned to the blanket laying on the floor in front of where her son sat. "If Kat left for good, like that note says, why didn't she take Danny's blanket?"

Viktor stared at her, trying to see the implications of what she was saying.

"It's not just the blanket. Everything Ysabel sent, for her, for the baby, she left it all here. Even the car seat. She didn't even take extra diapers."

Slowly Viktor's mind scrambled to catch up. "You're suggesting she didn't leave?"

"Not on her own. Or at least not for good. That's why I was hoping she rushed to catch up with you."

Viktor could feel his head nodding slowly, though his mind was racing at two hundred kilometers an hour. Taylor was right. Kat wouldn't have left empty-handed, without the most simple things she needed to keep the baby safe and comfortable. Which meant…where had she gone? And how was he going to find her?

He forced himself to take a deep breath. To not panic. To think. At least he wasn't alone in this. Really, in all of this, he'd never been alone. He just hadn't realized it until he came back to Houston.

All he had to do was ask for help.

KAT AWOKE with a searing pain in her shoulder and a headache that throbbed from the roots of her teeth to the ends of her hair. She didn't dare move her head. She didn't dare open her eyes. Underneath her, the firm softness of a mattress shifted with her weight.

What had happened?

She remembered Taylor leaving the apartment. Viktor's speech. The love she felt. The pride. She remembered holding Danny up to the TV. The ring of the buzzer. Then, everything fuzzy.

Danny.

A surge of adrenaline rifled through her, making her stomach queasy and her blood fire to life. She forced her eyes open, but her surroundings were as dark as when they were closed.

Something covered her mouth, sticky, strong. Rope cut into her wrists, tied behind her back. She couldn't move her legs.

Danny.

Someone had taken her, drugged her. Someone must have taken her baby, too. She shook her head, pain exploding along her neck at the movement. Danny had to be alive. He had to be okay.

He had to be.

Tears swamped her eyes, turning the darkness liquid. She had to think. If she gave into panic, she couldn't do her baby any good.

She forced herself to breathe. Deep breaths through her nose. One. Two. She could smell something…the light tickle of a scent…a scent she knew. Danny.

She swallowed the lump in her throat, the fear, the tears. She took another deep breath in.

The light smell of shampoo. The warm, soft skin. The tiniest hint of a diaper that needed changing. She'd only given birth to him a few scant days ago, but she knew those scents better than she knew any others.

Gritting her teeth, she rolled her body sideways on the bed, then let herself settle on her back once again. Her hands tingled sharply with the small taste of circulation, like needles sticking her skin.

She couldn't search the room if she couldn't feel her hands. With her hands tied behind her, she couldn't search the room at all. She needed to get them in front.

Pulling in another breath, she scootched her hands over her hips, over her butt. She moved inch by inch. Her shoulder screamed with the effort, her muscles stretching and pulling. Sweat broke out on her forehead and slicked her back and neck.

She'd heard pregnancy hormones softened the joints, made the ligaments and cartilage more flexible. She hoped their effects still held, at least a few days after the baby was born. She curled her spine, making her body as short as she could, and slid her hands down to her thighs and her legs through the loop of her arms.

For a few seconds she just lay still, breathing willing her stomach to keep control. Then she used the leverage of her legs to lift herself into a sitting position.

Her legs draped down, over the edge of the bed to the floor. She was in a house. A house with a bed. But as much as she willed her eyes to adjust to the darkness, she still couldn't see.

She turned her attention to the bed. Moving slowly, she smoothed her fingertips over the thick duvet of a light down comforter. She moved back and forth, as methodical as a search party in the woods. Her fingers touched something warm.

A whimper stuck in her throat.

She skimmed her fingertips over his wispy hair his little arms, his soft tummy, rising and falling with each breath. A light creaking sound rose in the darkness, the noise he made every time he woke up, as his lips opened round as an O and searched for something to eat.

Feeling his face with gentle fingers, she offered him a knuckle.

As relieved as she was to have her baby, to know he was alive and well, she knew it wouldn't last forever. Danny was the heir to the throne of

Rasnovia. And with Viktor's announcement that he would fight for his country, there was still a price on Danny's head.

She had to get him out of here. She had to escape. But how? Gagged and tied, she couldn't even manage to change the little guy's pants. She sure couldn't escape whatever place this was.

Cold settled over her skin, chill setting in after her exertion. She couldn't give up. She would find her way out. She just had to figure out how.

A low sound mixed with the beat of her pulse in her ears. The sound of voices. Male voices. Her captors? Or someone who could save her?

She held her breath and listened.

The voices were low, too low for her to pick out the words. But the tones...she knew the music of the voices...or at least one of them.

Viktor.

Fear kicked up her heartbeat once again, drowning out any further sound. If Viktor was here, was he searching for her? Or was he walking into a trap?

She called out as loudly as she could. The sound was muffled, but it was there. She screamed again. She roared until her throat started to feel shredded.

It wasn't enough. She needed something more. Something distinctive. A sound he would know.

She pulled her knuckle from Danny's mouth. He responded by fussing, that funny creaking sound.

Come on, Danny. Let's hear what you're made of.

She slipped her bound hands under him and jostled. She felt bad for doing this to the little guy, making him cry. It went against every instinct she had. But one instinct was stronger than that to comfort her son. The instinct to do whatever it took to save his life.

She bucked her hands underneath him. He broke into a cry. His agitation grew with each jab of her hands. His volume built until he was braying as loudly as his tiny voice could go.

Chapter Eighteen

Viktor stood just inside the beveled glass door of Deke's in-mansion bar and listened to the conversation in the foyer. The men's voices echoed off marble, amplifying their low mumble.

"I don't know what you're talking about," Deke said, his voice slightly slurred. "The last I saw him, he was in a courthouse surrounded by people like you."

When Viktor had arrived at the mansion, Deke was holding a crystal tumbler of scotch in his hand. No doubt he'd had a few before Viktor got there. He probably wasn't in the best shape to be fending off an FBI agent. Although Viktor appreciated the effort.

"It's imperative that I find him, Mr. Norton. Lives could depend on it."

Viktor took a step back, just to make sure he wasn't visible from the foyer. Special Agent Keller was right about one thing. Lives could depend on whether or not he was taken into FBI custody. The lives of Kat and Daniel. If he was tied up with the FBI, the way Flint and Jackson were, he wouldn't be able to find Kat. Not until it was too late.

If it wasn't too late already.

"Even if I knew where Viktor Romanov was, I wouldn't tell you. Not with the way law enforcement around here seems to be enforcing everything *but* the law. How do I know you aren't being paid off by the government of Rasnovia? How do I know you won't put a bullet in Viktor's brain as soon as you find him?"

"Mr. Norton, I can assure you…"

"You can assure my lawyers, that's what you can do."

A strange and very faint sound reached Viktor. Barely noticeable between the men's louder voices, it buzzed at the back of Viktor's mind like the whine of a mosquito.

"I would just like to talk to Prince Romanov."

"Talk. Sure. Like I said, my lawyers are very fond of talking."

Viktor squeezed his hands into fists, then released them. He hated hiding like this. Hated that he was putting Deke in this awkward position. And most of all, hated that he wasn't doing something to find Kat right this minute.

On the drive over to Deke's house, he'd heard on the radio Bobby Lee Stubfield had regained consciousness. The deputy recognized Kat at Taylor's house and reported Viktor as his attacker. Viktor had figured the law would be looking for him again. Although Viktor would expect someone from the county would be trying to track Viktor down for anything having to do with Stubfield. Not the FBI.

Apparently they were once again operating under the suspicion that he was a terrorist.

Viktor shook his head, that strange sound niggling at his ear. Did Deke have a cat? He couldn't imagine it. Maybe the animal belonged to one of his live-in servants.

"I'm acting on some information given to me by Flint McKade and Jackson Champion," Special Agent Keller went on.

Deke let out a laugh, though the sound seemed more tense than jovial. "What did they say?"

"I can't divulge that."

"Well, I can't divulge anything about the prince. Mostly because I don't know anything."

"Your chauffeur said he brought Prince Romanov to this address."

Viktor flinched inwardly. If he'd known the FBI were coming after him again, he would have been more careful in covering the tracks he'd left. As it was, he'd left a trail behind that glowed like a neon arrow.

"Why would a chauffeur of mine say that?"

"Did he drive the prince here?"

"Not that I'm aware of. And trust me, if he's hiring himself out while he's on my payroll, he won't be on that payroll long."

"So you're saying the prince isn't here?"

Another bark of a laugh from Deke. "And they say you FBI guys are slow to catch on."

"Do you mind if I come in and look around?"

"Yes. I mind. This is a twenty-eight-year-old single malt I'm drinking. I'd like to concentrate on it." Deke's voice soared in righteous indignation. "Now I'll lay out the choice for you slowly, so you'll understand. Either you get a warrant to search my home, or you let me enjoy the few sips I have left."

Silence stretched from the foyer, broken only by that strange mewing from somewhere in the giant house. Finally Keller cleared his throat. "Very well. But I know he's here, Mr. Norton. And as soon as I can prove it, I'll be back with that warrant."

The door thunked closed.

Viktor sagged back against the wall.

Deke's footsteps traced back toward him across the marble floor. "I don't know what your so-called Aggie Four friends told Special Agent Keller there, but it seems he's hot to talk to you."

He stepped into the bar. His voice was clear and strong now, and while Viktor had witnessed him drinking most of the tumbler of scotch in the minutes before the FBI agent arrived, he realized the drunken bit was just an act.

"Thanks, Deke. I owe you."

"Yes. You do, don't you?" Deke gave him a small smile, but he seemed agitated from his confrontation with the law.

Viktor couldn't blame him. When Deke had offered to help, he probably hadn't counted on having to put himself on the wrong side of the FBI. "I'll owe you even more if you can help me find Kat."

"Kat? The horse groom who came to see me?" He phrased it as a question, but Viktor got the distinct impression he already knew the truth.

"She's my fiancée."

"And the baby was yours."

"Yes. And he's missing, too."

Deke held up a hand. "Hold it right there. Maybe we can take care of this whole thing right now. I'll make some calls." He strode to the mahogany bar and picked up a cordless phone.

In the quiet, Viktor could still hear that faint sound. Not a cat. Not quite. But something familiar. Something he should be able to identify.

Deke punched a number into the phone and

held it to his ear. "I need you here right now. Yes. My house." He hit the off button and set the phone back on the bar.

"Lawyers?"

"Bodyguards. They double as investigators. There's a reason I know all the things I know."

Viktor nodded. Deke did seem to have knowledge others didn't share. How did Jackson put it? He had his finger on the pulse, or some such. Viktor just hoped his magic detectives would be able to find Kat. And fast. "How long until they get here?"

"Not long." Deke paced across the floor, his alligator boots thrumming in a steady rhythm. "You know, I've never understood The Aggie Four. Why just four? It seems the foundation would be able to get more done if there were more members."

Viktor shook his head. The last thing he wanted to talk was business. He wanted to move. Do something. Find Kat and Daniel *now*. But he supposed he could give Deke this. After all, he was going out of his way to help Viktor out. "We all see things the same way. We have the same philosophy about business. Power. Responsibility. That we have an obligation to do some good in the world, not just line our pockets."

"And others don't share those views?"

"Not too many that we've found."

"Not me? Is that what you're saying?"

Now it was Viktor's turn to lie. The truth was, Deke didn't quite fit in. He never had. He was a shrewd businessman, a great man to go to for any type of business advice. Extremely successful in his own right, certainly. But he didn't have quite the same dedication to the world, to the future as the others in The Aggie Four.

But Viktor couldn't admit that to Deke. "No. I'm not saying that. No."

"Then why was I never asked to join The Aggie Four?"

Viktor didn't know what to say. He walked across the room to the bar area to buy time. If he said the wrong thing, would Deke refuse to help find Kat? Would he be on his own again with the FBI breathing down his neck?

The sound seemed louder over here, as if it was filtering into the room through a heating duct above.

Viktor turned to face Deke. "I guess we never asked you because you were older. You seemed to have different priorities."

The doorbell chimed, echoing through the marble foyer.

Deke stared at him, a frown lining his brow, as if he wasn't thrilled with Viktor's answer. "My bodyguards are here. They'll take care of everything. That's what I pay them for." He turned for the foyer, leaving Viktor in silence.

Not silence.

The sound continued. Agitating. Grating at Viktor's nerves like the crying of a baby that can't be consoled.

The crying of a baby.

Viktor looked up at the heating grate. Danny? Kat? Somewhere in the house? But where? Why?

The conversation with Deke rolled through his mind. So like other conversations over the years. Always with a note of the hurt outsider. Always with a touch of resentment toward The Aggie Four and their work. Always with the feeling that Deke had one hand out to shake hands and the other behind his back holding a knife.

It was so clear. Right there in front of his face. Lawrence McElroy might be an investor in Trifecta, but he wasn't calling the shots. He never had been. And neither was Abdul Jabar. Neither man had the power. Neither man had the personal knowledge. No, the only man who fit the bill was the one Viktor had gone to for help. The man who'd paid off Bobby Lee Stubfield, the one who'd financed the coup in Rasnovia, the "friend" who'd engineered personal attacks on each member of The Aggie Four: Deke Norton.

Viktor rifled through the bar drawer. Grabbing a knife of his own, he made his way through the bar area and out a door leading to the next room.

Deke's mansion was huge, sprawling, easy to get lost in. But Viktor didn't want to get lost. He wanted to find Kat, Daniel, and he knew he was in the race of his life.

The men at the door weren't bodyguards. They were mercenaries. And as Deke said, they were here to take care of everything. Him. Kat. Daniel. But Viktor wouldn't allow it. He would take care of them first.

Or he would die trying.

KAT'S EYES BLURRED WITH TEARS. She heard sounds from outside the room. Footfalls. Voices. The house seemed to be filled with men, but minutes had passed without her hearing a single word from Viktor.

Was he still alive?

Screaming inside, she willed herself calm. Willed herself to think. If Viktor had been killed, if he wasn't coming to save them, she would have to figure out another way. She would have to make sure their son survived.

She moved her hands away from her crying little boy. Walking blindly to one side, she continued until she bumped into a wall. She skimmed bound hands along the papered surface. There had to be a door. A window. Something.

Her fingers hit the painted wood surface of a

molding, then skimmed over a solid door. She found the knob and tried it. Locked. So much for the easy option. She needed to find a window. Another way out.

Footfalls thundered in the hallway outside.

She ducked to the side of the door. Her foot hit something. A table. A lamp tilted precariously on the surface.

Not ideal, but it would have to do.

She grasped the lamp and lifted it, pulling its cord from the wall. It was heavy in her hands. Her damaged shoulder screamed as she lifted it.

The footfalls grew louder, rising over Danny's wail. The barks of men's voices added to the din.

The reality of what was about to happen hit her. It would take a miracle for her to get out of this. A miracle to save her son. To find Viktor, provided he was still alive. But no matter what happened in the next few minutes, she wasn't going to go down without a fight.

The doorknob rattled. A key grated in the lock. It swung open, the back of the door concealing her hiding spot. Light streamed in, over the bed, over her son's flailing arms and legs. A man stepped into the room.

And Kat attacked.

VIKTOR HEARD THE CRASH just as he rounded the corner of the third floor hall. A man's brutal voice erupted in a stream of obscenities. A woman screamed.

Kat.

He wanted to rush to her. Needed to. But he forced his feet to slow. The men ahead had guns. They were trained killers. And all that stood between Kat and Daniel and death was him, a diplomat armed with a paring knife.

He had to play this smart. Figure out a way to even the odds.

If only he could get the attention of the FBI. If only he hadn't let Deke send Keller away. But if-onlys got him nowhere. He had to think.

"Get against the wall," a brutal voice yelled.

Viktor's heart crowded high in his chest, beating wildly. An American, but not Deke. One of the mercenaries from D-Base.

Moving slowly, he rounded the corner and focused on the open door to the room ahead. He could see a man's combat boots lying at the edge of the room, as if he was sitting or prone on the floor.

"Not in here. Not in here. Take them somewhere. To a swamp, the gulf, I don't care. I just don't want them discovered," Deke shouted. "And find Romanov. Now!"

Viktor should run. Alert the FBI. But he couldn't leave Kat here with those men. And Daniel. They barely had to raise a finger to hurt Daniel.

He held the knife in front of him, forcing his hand not to shake. What he wouldn't give for a gun. To fight fire power with fire power. But he couldn't think about that now. He could only think about what he needed to do.

Save Kat. Save Daniel.

He tensed at the edge of the door. Waiting. Waiting.

A man stepped over the boots. He strode out of the room.

Viktor didn't think. He just lashed out. The knife sank into clothing, into soft flesh beneath.

The man screamed in agony and clutched at his chest.

Hand warm and wet with blood, Viktor stabbed again and again. The man lurched forward. He fell to the floor, Viktor's knife buried in his stomach.

"Kat!" He sprang past the man, through the door.

Kat stood near the bed, hands bound, eyes wide with fear. "Watch—"

Something clubbed him from behind. The butt of a gun. His head rattled. He fell to his hands and knees. His vision threatened to go dark.

"Viktor?" Her voice sounded tear soaked, but gained in strength. "Viktor."

"Don't move," Deke commanded. He held his

hand out in front of him, toward Kat. And in his fist was a gun.

Viktor gritted his teeth, forced his mind to clear. "Back off, Kat."

"You'd better listen to the prince," Deke taunted. "After all, that was a royal order."

A boot plowed into Viktor's ribs.

Breath whooshed from his lungs. Pain ripped through his chest. He slumped to the floor and gasped for oxygen.

"That feel good, Prince? How about another?"

Blows racked Viktor, his chest, his stomach, his head. His head ached to high heaven. The copper tang of blood filled his mouth. He struggled to get up only to crumple under another blow.

"Look at the mess you've made. How am I going to explain this?"

"Stop!" Kat screamed.

The kicks kept coming. All of Deke's frustrations raining down on him. "I only wanted to be part of things. The Aggie Four Foundation. Rasnovia. You only had to ask. You only had to include me, show me some respect. But you couldn't do that. None of you could. Well, now you see. I'm a very wealthy man. I'm a powerful man. I had your family killed, and now I'll kill you. But before you die, I want you to know that by the time I'm finished, I'm going to own everything The Aggie Four holds dear. Rasnovia is already mine. Champion Shipping is living on a prayer. And eventually I'll have the ranch and the auction house and every single damn thing The Aggie Four owns."

"Stop!"

Viktor could make out movement through swollen eyes. Kat. She hurled her body across the room. Throwing herself at Deke...*and the gun in his hand.*

An explosion rocked the room. The smell of gunpowder blanketed the air.

Deke shot Kat. He shot— Viktor lurched up, to his hip, to his knees.

No. She was still on her feet. Still fighting. Clawing at Deke's face with her nails like a lioness. The baby wailed from the bed.

Deke backhanded her, sending her flying.

But Viktor had him. His hand closed around Deke's hand, around the handle of the pistol. He fought, trying to wrench it from Deke's grasp, but Deke wouldn't give.

Something stirred from behind Viktor. A soldier. *"Viktor!"*

He swung around, taking the gun and Deke's hand with him. He fitted his finger over Deke's and pulled the trigger.

The explosions were deafening. One. Two. The soldier fell.

Deke struggled for control. For the gun. For life.

Viktor's head throbbed. His pulse thundered in his ears. He struggled to breathe, pain raging like fire in his chest. Darkness clouded the edges of his vision. Darkness he couldn't push away.

The sharp crack of gunfire ripped the room once again. And then everything went black.

KAT DROPPED THE GUARD'S gun and raced to Viktor. He was still tangled with Deke. Their hands joined, clutching Deke's gun, even as the life drained from Deke's gray eyes and his blood soaked into the carpet. Danny's wail continued from the bed.

She clutched Viktor's shoulder with still-bound hands and rolled him onto his back. He was heavy. Dead weight. His head lolled to the side.

"Viktor?" Her mouth went dry. Her heart squeezed with each thunderous beat. She placed her fingers on his cheek, turning his face to her. "Viktor? You have to be okay. You have to."

A crash sounded from somewhere downstairs. Male shouts echoed through the mansion. More soldiers.

Kat looked down at her prince, at her love. So this is how it would end? Their dreams for

Rasnovia? Their partnership? Their family? Was this all that was left?

She lowered her lips to Viktor's and took one last kiss.

His lips moved against hers. Still warm. Breath from his nose caressed her cheek. He was still alive. Still with her. And she knew what she needed to do.

She rose on unsteady feet. Bending down, she picked up the soldier's gun, the one she'd used to shoot Deke, the one she'd dropped. She'd continue to fight. She wouldn't give up. And if by some miracle they got out of this alive, she would keep on and on until all their dreams were fulfilled. She'd always longed for something bigger, something more. And now she was faced with it.

No matter what happened, she wasn't going to back down.

She pointed the gun toward the door. Footsteps drew closer. Quiet voices. There were a lot of them, she could tell. Although they were stealthy, they sounded like an army. She didn't stand a chance, and she knew it. The sounds of them swarmed through the house from floor to floor. They mounted the stairs to the third floor. They gathered in the hall outside.

And then they were in the room.

"Get on the floor! Get on the floor! Put the gun down! Police!"

The last word washed over Kat and lodged in her mind. Could she trust them? Could she trust any of them?

"It's okay, Kat. Put it down. We won." His voice was quiet, barely more than a whisper, but it was the sweetest sound she'd ever heard. She set the gun on the floor and collapsed into Viktor's arms.

Epilogue

Standing at the cathedral's ornate flower-swagged altar, Viktor wished he'd done things differently.

Not as far as his legal troubles went. They'd been resolved more quickly than he'd believed possible. And as for Rasnovia, with Deke dead and their money supply gone, the rebels' government collapsed before Christmas, taking Rasnovia's economy with it. But The Aggie Four, joining with other investors, had gotten the country back on its feet and running. And although they weren't back to the heights they'd reached before the coup, the country was on its way.

He also had no regrets regarding the wedding plans. The church in Rasnovia's capital city was beautiful, filled with so many roses and lilies, the air was sweet with each breath. As per Rasnovian tradition, the bride and groom form a new family, one composed of friends who will support them in their married life. For Viktor and Kat, that choice was easy. And as he looked at each of his groomsmen, Flint, Akeem and Jackson, and their beaming smiles, he felt pride welling in his chest.

Walking down the aisle, Ysabel led the way, her gown svelte over her post-baby figure, although Jackson had told him before the ceremony they were already planning their second child.

After her came Taylor, who was now bearing, not Akeem's child—not yet—but his wedding band. And once her new accounting business was more established, she'd promised they'd start working on giving Christopher that little brother he wanted to wrestle with so much.

The maid of honor was Lora Leigh, the waddle in her gait as she walked the aisle suggesting the baby would come any day. Not that she'd stopped working with the horses. But at Flint's insistence, she'd taken on a more advisory role.

In front of the church sat Ilona's four children, safe and whole and now living in the palace with Viktor and Kat. And although they were still struggling with all they'd lost, just as the rest of the Rasnovian people were, they were a strong and brave testament to a new generation. A generation ready to embrace peace and democracy.

No, the wedding was perfect, and the celebration afterwards, which would last for two additional days at the newly restored palace, promised to be more than grand. A reception fit for a queen.

The mistake Viktor had made was not with politics or close friends in the wedding party or the pomp and circumstance of a traditional Rasnovian royal wedding. It was that he should have gotten more help for Kat's mother and poor Lucinda, although Christopher was doing his best. Daniel and Jackson and Ysabel's little girl, on the other hand, weren't quite so cooperative.

And so it was, amid baby babbling and fussing, that the Rasnovian wedding march filled the arched ceiling of the cathedral and the bride started the last steps of her journey to become queen.

Viktor sucked in a breath as she stepped into the aisle on her father's arm.

She looked every inch the royal, from her traditional crown of flowers and colorful ribbons to her Rasnovian wedding gown, sparkling with strands of diamonds set into the dress itself.

But the only diamonds Viktor cared about were the ones adorning the bands on her finger, the ones he would change from the left hand to the right when the ceremony was over.

When they were officially partners, once and for all. King and queen. Husband and wife.

* * * * *

Don't miss Ann Voss Peterson's next
Harlequin Intrigue book,
COVERT COOTCHIE-COOTCHIE-COO,
on sale in September 2009!

In honor of our 60th anniversary,
Harlequin® American Romance®
is celebrating by featuring an all-American
male each month, all year long with
MEN MADE IN AMERICA!
This June, we'll be featuring American men
living in the West.

Here's a sneak preview of
THE CHIEF RANGER
by Rebecca Winters.

*Chief Ranger Vance Rossiter has to confront the
sister of a man who died while under Vance's
watch...and also confront his attraction to her.*

"Chief Ranger Rossiter?" The sight of the woman who'd stepped inside Vance's office brought him to his feet. "I'm Rachel Darrow. Your secretary said I should come right in."

"Please," he said, walking around his desk to shake her hand. At a glance he estimated she was in her midtwenties. Her feminine curves did wonders for the pale blue T-shirt and jeans she was wearing. "Ranger Jarvis informed me there's a young boy with you."

The unfriendly expression in her beautiful green eyes caught him off guard. "Yes," was her clipped reply. "When we arrived in Yosemite the ranger told me I couldn't go anywhere in the park until I talked to you first."

"That's right."

"Knowing you wanted this meeting to be private, he offered to show my nephew around Headquarters."

So this woman was the victim's sister…. "What's his name?"

"Nicky."

The boy who haunted Vance's dreams now had a name. "How old is he?"

"He turned six three weeks ago. Were you the man in charge when my brother and sister-in-law were killed?"

"Yes. To tell you I'm sorry for what happened couldn't begin to convey my feelings."

The woman's gaze didn't flicker. "I won't even try to describe mine. Just tell me one thing. Was their accident preventable?"

"Yes," he answered without hesitation.

"In other words, the people working under you fell asleep on your watch and two lives were snuffed out as a result."

Hearing it put like that, he had to set the record straight. "My staff had nothing to do with it. I, myself, could have prevented the loss of life."

Ms. Darrow's expression hardened. "So you admit culpability."

"Yes. I take full blame."

A look of pain crossed over her features. "You can just stand there and admit it?" Her cry echoed that of his own tortured soul.

"Yes." He sucked in his breath.

"I work for a cruise line. Aboard ship, it's the

captain's responsibility to maintain rigid safety regulations. If a disaster like that had happened while he was in charge he would have been relieved of his command and never given another ship again."

Rachel Darrow couldn't know she was preaching to the converted. "If you've come to the park with the intention of bringing a lawsuit against me for negligence, maybe you should." It would only be what he deserved.

"Maybe I will."

In the next instant, she wheeled around and hurried out of his office. Vance could have gone after her, but it would cause a scene, something he was loath to do for a variety of reasons. In the first place, he needed to cool down before he approached her again.

The discovery of the Darrows' frozen bodies had affected every ranger in the park. A little boy had been orphaned—a boy whose aunt was all he had left.

* * * * *

Will Rachel allow Vance to explain—
and will she let him into her heart?
Find out in
THE CHIEF RANGER
Available June 2009 from
Harlequin® American Romance®.

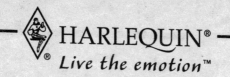

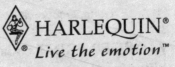

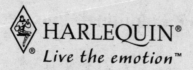

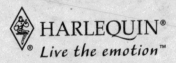

Harlequin® Historical
Historical Romantic Adventure!

*Imagine a time of chivalrous
knights and unconventional ladies,
roguish rakes and impetuous
heiresses, rugged cowboys
and spirited frontierswomen—
these rich and vivid tales will
capture your imagination!*

*Harlequin Historical . . .
they're too good to miss!*

HARLEQUIN®
Presents

The world's bestselling romance series...
The series that brings you your favorite authors,
month after month:

Helen Bianchin...Emma Darcy
Lynne Graham...Penny Jordan
Miranda Lee...Sandra Marton
Anne Mather...Carole Mortimer
Melanie Milburne...Michelle Reid

and many more talented authors!

Wealthy, powerful, gorgeous men...
Women who have feelings just like your own...
The stories you love, set in exotic, glamorous locations...

HARLEQUIN®
Presents

Seduction and Passion Guaranteed!

HPDIR08

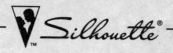

SPECIAL EDITION™

Emotional, compelling stories that capture the intensity of living, loving and creating a family in today's world.

Modern, passionate reads that are powerful and provocative.

nocturne

Dramatic and sensual tales of paranormal romance.

Romantic SUSPENSE

Romances that are sparked by danger and fueled by passion.

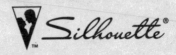